Before my toes touched the ground, he had swept me into his arms for a heady embrace. It was no mere kiss, but a crushing assault on all my senses. The kind of kiss a woman dreams of, alone at night. It was the kiss of a bandit or a pirate, demanding and wild, hot on the lips, and setting the blood singing. I heard the leaves above whisper in the breeze, smelled the sweet scent of wild flowers and the more pungent aroma of the horses to remind me it was real and not a dream . . . .

STRANGE CAPERS

Joan Smith

FAWCETT CREST • NEW YORK

A Fawcett Crest Book
Published by Ballantine Books
Copyright © 1986 by Joan Smith

Library of Congress Catalog Card Number: 86-91178

ISBN 0-449-20761-7

Manufactured in the United States of America

First Edition: October 1986

We that are true lovers run into strange capers.

—WILLIAM SHAKESPEARE
As You Like It, Act II, Scene 4

STRANGE CAPERS

CHAPTER ONE

RACHEL, LADY SAVAGE, WAS A SCOUNDREL AND A THIEF. In deference to her social position she was called a "clever, managing woman," but this was sheer euphemism. She was the most larcenous lady who ever made her curtsies at St. James's. She even stole her husband from another lady, but did it before he got to the altar with his first love so that her marauding tactic was not indictable. Once shackled to John Savage, she blackmailed some highly placed friends into obtaining a knighthood for him, and, much more important, the right to call herself Lady Savage. The house in which she resides on the southeast coast of England was wangled out of her cousin, Lord Aiglon, by a wicked piece of subterfuge. When Sir John died of weariness from trotting to keep up with his lady ten years ago, Rachel went in tears to Lord Aiglon and threw herself on his bosom.

I wasn't acquainted with Rachel at the time, but I'd be willing to wager that she went in rags and tatters and billeted herself on him in London till he finally turned Thornbury over to be rid of her. As to myself, she stole me from my home in Kent. Sir John was Mama's brother. When I tell you I am the eldest of four girls and two boys, you will realize she met with little opposition to her scheme. I was initially invited to visit her at Thornbury for one summer, the invitation dropping hints of the superior company I would meet, the salubrious sea breezes, the change of scene, but not a single word to indicate that Thornbury was a decaying shambles of a place with too few servants and a great deal of work to be done.

I never escaped from Rachel. My return home was put off so many times that at last it ceased to be spoken of at all, and I became a part of the little Thornbury household. Fortunately, I rub along with Rachel and like her despite those foibles that have alienated so many of her family.

The scheme that occupied her dishonest mind in the summer I write of was the accumulation of sufficient funds to have a holiday in London. This was to occur the following spring, and the excuse for it was to present her niece, Isabel Godwin, to society. Isabel's mama, Rachel's own sister, was I can only assume a deal less capable than Rachel in managing her affairs.

"Aiglon, I am sure, will be happy to let us use his London residence as a pied-à-terre for one Season," Rachel said firmly. "It is the least he can do for his cousin. God knows he has done little enough else. This shabby place," she said, casting a disparaging eye around her saloon, "is scarcely fit to live in. I shall write and tell Riddell we need a carpet for the front stairs."

Riddell was in charge of minor business affairs for Lord Aiglon, and was vigorously courted by Lady Savage though she had never actually met the man. "I shall ask how his mama goes on. She has the gout, you remember he mentioned in his last letter."

"Flu, Rachel," I reminded her. "It was the flu Mrs. Riddell had."

"I believe you're right. How very clever you are, to be sure. Then we shall put the blue carpet from the spare guest room on the stairs. Willard can cut it into strips and tack it in place. The guest room is useless in any case, with the canopies rotted into decay and removed."

I glanced to the saloon curtains (*née* bed canopy) and noticed they were not far from moldering. I had not thought it worth the effort last year to make them from the guest-room canopy, but at the time I was unaware that she had gotten fifty guineas from Riddell for new ones. Rachel has *some* conscience. She would generally move old furniture or hangings out when she took money to purchase new ones. Other than the dovecote, for which she got a hundred pounds and supplied absolutely nothing, she usually had something she could show her unwitting patron if ever he should chance to visit her.

"If Lord Aiglon ever drops in on us, Rachel, we are undone. Revealed as the criminals we—*you* are."

At this Rachel's nose pulled down into her chin. This tactic strengthens my hope that she has some vestige of a conscience. Rachel's nose is not really overlarge, but it seems to be placed rather lower on her face than other people's noses, and slides lower yet when she feels guilty or displeased. Her eyes are brown and wide-spaced. The combination of these features gives her face an equine cast, though I do not mean to say that she is downright ugly. Merely she is not pretty. She has nice brown hair that is honey colored when the sun shines on it. She is tall, thin, and extremely elegant. There is no expensive flamboyance to her wardrobe, but the few outfits she does possess are unexceptionable—of good quality and materials and fine workmanship. Rachel is the sort of woman who "found an excellent little French modiste" who conjures up gowns at low cost.

"There is no fear of Aiglon's coming," she replied. "He has never once been here in the decade since I took over the running of Thornbury for him. He is a sorry fel-low, what they call in London a Corinthian. A pity to think he inherited all the Aiglon estates, but the family does not believe in splintering. It is quite understood, however, that the head of the family looks after those less fortunate. Like me," she added, lest her meaning had escaped me.

"No, I shouldn't think he'd be able to leave London if he wanted to. Now that he is with the Foreign Office, he would be busy. Especially at this time," I added.

The reason "this time" was particularly demanding had to do with the fear of Bonaparte's invasion. We were more aware of it than most, situated as we were on the east coast where he would be most likely to land, though the whole of England was readying its defenses. One assumed the Foreign Office would be in a state of hysteria, and thus Bonaparte's possible invasion saved us at least from Lord Aiglon's equally fearsome invasion of his own estate.

"I shall just dash my note off to Riddell about the stair carpet, Constance, and then you and I shall trot it into the village. Ask Willard to lift the guest-room carpet and give it a sound beating before he installs it on the stairway. The bit that is under the bed must go at the bottom, where it will show. The rest of the staircase is so dark it would be a waste to put new carpeting there," she rationalized. Perhaps such managing skills deserved a reward, but I *did* feel guilty for her.

Rachel trotted off to the study and I went in search of our factotum, Willard. I found him polishing the little crystal pendants that decorate a pair of wall lamps in the front hall. Willard was about seventy years old, frightfully stooped at the shoulders, but a willing slave to Rachel, whom he adored. No one, he told me, cared that Thornbury was falling into ruin—till Rachel came. Apparently Willard deemed such renovations as switching mildewed curtains from one room to another to be high style. One could only wonder what the place was like before she arrived.

"Oh, aye," he said, nodding his head. "That'll be grand, a carpet on the front staircase. We'll be the talk of the neighborhood. I'll just give the rug a bit of a beating, slice her up, and lay her down. It'll be done in no time." In fact, it would involve a few days' work and a deal of hammering and pounding, but Willard always disavowed the difficulty of his efforts like the good slave he was.

I left the front hall and went up the uncarpeted stairs to my room to make ready for the jaunt into Folkestone. Dover was just as close, but the prices were a little higher there, so we had fallen into the habit of considering Folkestone "our" town.

Living in rural isolation, with our closest neighbor a mile away, we make much of a trip to town. Any excuse is good enough, and we usually find at least two a week, sometimes more. But no matter how often we go, we prepare a careful toilette. I brushed my dark brown curls from my forehead, vainly admiring their red highlights that glinted in the sun. Any lady in the land could rhyme off her "best feature," and I would not hesitate a moment to call my chestnut hair mine. I don't actively dislike my eyes either: hazel in color, of decent size and reasonably lashed. For the rest, I wish I could hang a veil below my eyes and hide my nose and mouth like a Muslim woman. But then the veil would protrude rather far. In other words, my nose is not small. It is a well-shaped nose and would look unexceptionable on a gentleman. I can't decide whether it is an added misfortune or a benefit that I have a mouth and jaw large enough to balance it. Mickey Dougherty, the local flirt, tells me I am handsome. As no one has ever told me I am beautiful, or even pretty, I cherish his description.

I set a bonnet, carefully chosen to reveal as much as possible of my best feature, on my head, tilted it over my eye, and put on my dark green pelisse. I was quite satisfied with my outfit till I reached the landing and looked at

Rachel. I always looked unkempt beside her. She was such an authoritarian, she had every hair on her head under complete control. It sat like silk, smooth and shiny, and her navy pelisse was similarly perfect. Her gloves, which I know for a fact are three years old, looked brand-new. She was fingering one of the little crystal pendants Willard had been polishing.

"Pretty little thing," she said with that light in her eyes that denotes a scheme. What she hoped to do with the pendants was beyond me.

We went out the front door, where the gig awaited our pleasure. Willard couldn't be in two places at once, so when he was busy at home, we found the weather to be of a kind that lured us into the gig. A fairly stiff ocean breeze made it necessary for me to hold on to my bonnet and pelisse, but Rachel's behaved themselves perfectly while she handled the ribbons in the same manner.

It was lively on the coast that spring. Martello towers had sprung up, and guards patroled back and forth. There was a regiment of soldiers in barracks performing maneuvers, and in towns and villages the militia, too, was practicing. Many a telescope was trained on the Channel, looking to see if Napoleon was crossing in his flat-bottomed boats. It was considered more likely, of course, that he'd come by night, and for that purpose furze stacks were placed at mile intervals, ready to be lit in case of invasion. They were the signal to chime the church bells in a prescribed and menacing way that would alert the citizens to danger.

All this military activity in no way interfered with the usual fishing, coastal shipping, or even pleasure-boating. I noticed Mickey Dougherty's lugger was out. Here on the coast the swift and maneuverable three-masted luggers are highly suspect. They are commonly used for smuggling.

Rachel took a sharp look at Mickey's boat, and her lips pulled down in dismay.

"Post the note to Aiglon for me, Constance, if you don't mind. I'll nip in to see Madame Bieler while I'm in town," Rachel said.

"You think Mickey's brought in some new silks?" I asked blandly.

It was generally understood, though never actually said, that Madame's inexplicable supply of silks came from France via Mickey's lugger.

"Very likely, but it's a wee bottle of brandy for Willard I have in mind. He'll be tuckered out after installing the new carpet on the stairs. Willard earns his keep. You might check to see if there's anything for us at the post office as well."

When we went to Folkestone, we did not visit the tourist area of town known as the Leas. This area stretches along the clifftop for over a mile and offers an excellent view of the sea and a purplish-blue haze that we called France. Of more interest to shoppers is the old fishing town that extends down to the harbor and contains, among other things, Madame Bieler's shop.

I left Rachel and went to the post office, where a delightful surprise awaited me. I had received a letter from home. Rachel had three letters, one bearing Aiglon's crest. I judged from its light weight that no folding money or bank draft was enclosed. I assumed it was from Riddell and that he was refusing some past request. This was all to the good. Rachel requested many items that she knew would be denied, but after several refusals Riddell usually acceded to some demand.

With the letters in my reticule, I strolled along the main street looking in shop windows and enjoying the bustle of activity till I came to Madame Bieler's discreet sign. I learned from Madame's assistant that Lady Savage was not there. She had been in and had already left. I glanced up and down the street looking for her, and was surprised to see her coming out of an old used-book shop. Rachel is not a great reader of anything but social columns and fashion magazines, yet she had a parcel in hand, and it wasn't the wee bottle for Willard. That would be in her reticule.

Just as I caught her eye and began crossing the street, Mickey Dougherty came strolling along toward her. Mickey was a handsome addition to the town. It hasn't many young bachelors to offer, and none who looked as fine as Mickey. He's a strapping six-footer with blue-black hair and a pair of laughing blue eyes that have ruined more than one woman. With no honest job and no money of his own, he manages to keep up an excellent appearance and drives the finest horses in the county. The fact that this disreputable gentleman has a foothold in society is due to his mother, Lady Ware. She used to be the plain Mrs. Dougherty from Ireland, but when her husband died she married an aging baron, Lord Ware, and moved herself and her son into his estate west of town.

"Good day to you, ladies," Mickey said, lifting his hat. I could swear his brogue becomes stronger by the year. "What brings the ladies of Thornbury into town?" His eyes, as he spoke, were laughing in Rachel's direction, not mine.

Rachel was beyond the time of life when a handsome young bachelor smiled on her in real pleasure. I, on the other hand, was accustomed to his flirtation and felt a little miffed that I was not receiving it. It meant no more to me than a passing breeze, but it was a small pleasure I had grown accustomed to.

"Oh, Mickey, I thought I saw your boat out in the water just a moment ago" was Rachel's answer.

"You did, surely. At least it should be on its way home by now. I climbed off down at the harbor and came for a

8

strut through town in hopes of pleasuring my eyes with a sight of you."

Rachel looked just a trifle nervous somehow, which was ridiculous. My attention to the interchange between the two of them increased. I noticed that Mickey was looking from the old used-bookstore to Rachel to the parcel in her hands, and his smile stretched a shade wider. "Planning a cozy evening reading by the fireside, are you? What book is it you've bought, Lady Savage?"

"A Bible," she answered curtly, and clutched the book more tightly.

This was patent nonsense. She already had a Bible, and if she had never seen one in her life, she wouldn't *buy* one.

"A Bible, is it? I'm very much interested in old Bibles myself. Could I have a look at it then?"

"No, I'm afraid we're in a bit of a hurry today, Mickey," Lady Savage answered. "Come along, Constance. Willard will be waiting for us."

"The, ah, *Bible* is for Willard, is it?" Mickey asked in a mischievous voice. "He's a blessing, is Willard. There's a man who'd do anything he was told to, milady, and no questions asked. But you *will* just bear in mind, won't you, that it's myself who mentioned to you the riches to be found in the Good Book?" He turned to me then, his eyes fairly dancing in mockery. "And have you taken up Bible reading as well, Constance, my love?"

"I'm a devout reader," I answered swiftly, hoping he would speak on to reveal what he was talking about.

"Aye, of every foolish novel that comes out."

"Come along, Constance," Rachel repeated, and took my arm to leave. Her pace was not much short of running.

I was entirely mystified, for in the usual way it takes a good deal more than a Mickey Dougherty to disconcert Rachel. She didn't dally for a minute in any of the other stores, either, but went straight to the hotel for the gig.

9

When we were seated in it, I asked her what Mickey had been talking about.

"Who knows what that rattle has in his mind?" she answered sharply, but the sharpness was meant for Mickey, not me.

"What did you really buy in that shop? I know it wasn't a Bible," I replied.

"Just an old history book about this area. It has some references to Thornbury in it. I thought I might send it as a gift to Lord Aiglon to put him in a giving mood."

"I see," I answered, though I didn't see at all.

She had never felt it necessary to oil him like this before. Why was she doing it now? Of course there was the projected stay in London. That might account for it. I had never heard that Aiglon was the least interested in history, but then an old book was the sort of thing whose price was indefinite. She'd pay a few pennies and offer it as a priceless antique.

"Was it Mickey who discovered the book?" I asked.

"Yes, he mentioned seeing it to me last Sunday. Actually, he said he planned to buy it himself, and was a little put out that I beat him to it."

This sounded completely plausible. It was the very sort of trick for which Rachel was famous. I accepted her word for it—in my guileless and innocent fashion—forgetting that she was such an accomplished thief. I thought it was only the book she had snitched from Mickey's fingers. As I look back on it, I remember that Rachel was particularly talkative during the remainder of that trip. She chattered like a magpie about nothing in particular. She distracted me, and she must have been very distracted herself, too, for she didn't think to ask me for her mail.

It wasn't till we were home and having our tea that I remembered her letters and gave them to her. She opened and read two of hers while I read mine from home. It was

Prissy who had written to me. She is only one year younger than myself and the closest to me in temperament. I felt some lonesomeness as I read of the family's doings. I would go home when Rachel went to London next spring, and if Prissy married the young man whose description filled two pages, I would stay at home. My two brothers were at school now, and the house would be less full. I could be useful there.

I was startled out of my ruminative state by a strangled ''Aagh!'' from Rachel. I looked in alarm to see she was reading the letter bearing Aiglon's frank.

''What's the matter? Is someone dead?'' I asked. Her face, an alarming shade of red, faded before my very eyes to rose, to pink, to bone-white.

''Worse!'' she managed to choke out. ''Aiglon is coming to Thornbury!''

I suspect my own color faded just as rapidly. ''When?'' I asked.

''Tomorrow.''

We exchanged a guilty stare. I felt an urge to jump up from the table and run and hide. Rachel must have felt even more culpable, but such was her sangfroid that she only called out ''Willard'' in a little fainter voice than usual.

CHAPTER TWO

RACHEL IS REALLY A MARVEL OF EFFICIENCY. EVEN BE-
fore Willard came shuffling into the room, she had recovered her wits sufficiently to begin laying plans and
preparing strategies to cover her larceny.

"The carpet for the front stairs must be the first matter
of business," she said.

"Leave it, Rachel. You posted that note asking for
money only today. He won't expect to see it done yet," I
advised.

Her nose pulled downward as she braced herself to confess the whole. "Actually, I said I had had it done already
and enclosed a bill. He will have received my letter before
he leaves tomorrow. He says he will be arriving around
dinnertime. Aiglon will be driving his curricle in this season—fifteen miles an hour, over the sixty-mile drive. We
shall have to give Willard a hand with the laying of it."

"How are we to make it look new?" I asked.

"We'll keep the lights low," she said, glancing again
at the troublesome letter.

"Why is he coming? Is there some special reason?"

"To rusticate—he wants no company. Well, that's
something at least. He won't be expecting a round of par-

ties. He's having his yacht sent down. That looks like a longish visit . . ."

"Rachel, about the dovecote," I reminded her. That loomed in my mind as the worst of her schemes, but she had her explanation for it in the twinkling of an eye.

"Vandals. Vandals knocked it down, and it was such a mess we just had the stones hauled away. There is that pile of stones at the back of the garden where half the dry wall fell down five years ago. The sea gulls made such depradations on the doves' eggs that we decided the coast was no proper place for a dovecote. What else? The saloon curtains were paid for over a year ago, so their condition can be explained by the malign sea air."

"What room will you put him in? The blue guest room would be the likeliest spot if it had curtains and a canopy. The other guest rooms are small."

"Yes, we have the best rooms ourselves, those with a view of the sea. I really think . . . Would you mind terribly to remove to the little yellow room at the back, Constance? It will only be for a week or so."

"Of course I don't mind. It is Aiglon's own house after all, but he must plan to stay longer than a week if he's having his yacht sent down," I pointed out.

"Longer? We'll be rid of him in three days," she prophesied merrily, and laughed.

There was a febrile excitement about her during that meal, which I put down to Aiglon's visit. God knows it would have been enough to put any ordinary person into spasms of fright, but I think now that the visit wasn't the cause of it at all. Looking back, it seemed a happy or anticipatory sort of excitement.

The thing I remember most about that night is helping Willard haul the blue carpet downstairs and hang it on the clothesline at about nine o'clock. Rachel, who took a supervisory position, had lights fixed in the backyard to allow

Willard and the servants to beat the carpet into newness. While they beat, I measured the front stairs, and when the carpet was as clean as a fifteen-year-old carpet with several grease stains could be, we laid it in the saloon and cut it into strips. Before any of us were allowed to lay our heads on our pillows that night, we had to install it. There was a tremendous commotion of hammering and running for sharper knives and scissors to cut through the thick rug. Willard's spirit was willing but his forearm was weak, so the stable boy and I ended up wielding the hammer. Other than the strange bellying at the curve of the stairs where we couldn't get it to lay flat, it didn't look too bad. Certainly not new, but not bad. At one o'clock in the morning, the job was done, and we were allowed to retire with the reminder to meet at seven in the morning to begin last-minute preparations.

Bleary-eyed and stiff, and with a throbbing thumb where the hammer had hit me, I straggled upstairs to bed. It was only after I lay down that I wondered why Aiglon was coming to Thornbury at this time. His being with the Foreign Office made me wonder if he was to take some part in the anti-Napoleon preparations. On that score, I wasn't unhappy to have an able-bodied man in the house. There were wicked stories circulating in the neighborhood as to how French soldiers treated their victims—especially female victims. Of course Aiglon was a lord and a government official, and this might induce the French to treat his household with some latitude. On the other hand, the French had a particular hatred of the nobility.

I reviewed what I knew about Aiglon from having heard him spoken of for five years. His real country seat was in Hampshire, not Sussex. It was called Westleigh and, according to rumor, was a magnificent heap. If he wanted to rusticate, why did he not go there? All my thoughts confirmed that he was coming on military business. Although he was invariably spoken of as a fashionable rake and rattle, it seemed to me that his having taken a government position showed there was more to him than that. It was spoken of as an important position as well, some sort of liaison work between the government and the military.

I also knew that Aiglon was a bachelor, though he had skated near the edge of engagement with a few ladies since I'd come to Thornbury. I, a fairly poor connection, was not in the least hopeful that he would become so enamored of me during his brief visit that any romance would develop. But if he turned out to be handsome, a pleasant flirtation was not impossible. It was on this stray wisp of a happy thought that I finally slept.

I believe Rachel slept even more poorly than myself. I heard her door open at some time during the night. It was raining and pitch black outside. I wondered what detail she had remembered and risen out of her bed to attend to. I heard her tiptoe past my room, but she hadn't lit a candle. She went downstairs, and I fell asleep again before she returned.

The first thing I noticed when I opened my eyes was the sodden, gray sky. Perhaps Aiglon will delay his visit, I thought optimistically. I didn't know him then, and thus had no way of suspecting his single-mindedness once he had set his course of action.

The rest of the day was one of busy, organized confusion. I had to remove all my personal effects from my room and take them across the hall to the yellow guest room. That done, I gave Aiglon's room a good cleaning with beeswax and turpentine until the furniture gleamed. Meg, the kitchen girl, was set to sweeping the carpet with tea leaves sprinkled to keep down the dust. Rachel spent some time in the kitchen overseeing a feast to tempt the palate of a London rattle. I was assigned the job of setting the table for dinner. I enjoyed that, but having to go out into

15

the garden to cull flowers in the pouring rain was less pleasant. I was a little annoyed to notice that one of the servants had made free with my waterproof coat and pattens. The coat was still damp and had mud splattered around the hem. I mentioned this to Rachel in passing when she came to approve the dinner table.

"You mustn't blame Meg, Constance. Actually, I borrowed it myself," she admitted. "The roses look a bit skimpy, don't you think?" she asked, surveying the centerpiece. She rooted in the basket of discards and stuck a few pieces of greenery amidst the blooms. "There, that's better."

"What are you serving, Rachel?" I asked. I was a little miffed that she'd worn my coat and gotten it dirty when she might as easily have put on her own. But that, I suspect, is the secret of her elegance. Her clothes are protected from rough wear.

She named an assortment of delicacies: turbot, fowl, a ham, and side dishes. While she spoke, I found myself wondering when she had been out and why. I asked about it, but she gave me her annoyed mare's look. "I went to put a few stones where the dovecote used to be," she answered. She is such a clever liar that she couches all of her remarks as if to indicate that the lie is a fact. The dovecote was never anywhere but in her mind and in a letter to Riddell.

"You got mud on the hem of my coat," I said.

"Give it to Meg to clean."

Meg had so much to do that I took the coat upstairs myself. I noticed that the mud on the inner side had hardened to blobs of earth. It was still wet on the outside, as I had worn it to cut flowers, but along the inner hem it was bone dry. I must have accused Rachel unjustly. That mud had been there for hours. It must have been there overnight. At the time, I had no reason to suspect that Rachel's nocturnal ramble had taken her outdoors in my coat, and she certainly didn't say so. I was privy to most of her crimes, but this one she had kept to herself. Only Willard knew what she was up to, and Willard would gladly have gone to the stake before he'd say a word against Lady Savage.

As the afternoon wore on, orders flew like sparks from Rachel's lips, and the servants, including myself, hopped to execute them. A fire was laid in the grate; wine was poured into decanters and one was taken to Aiglon's room; lamps unwittingly lit too close to the old-new stair carpet were extinguished; other saloon lamps were adjusted, moved, and moved again to allow some rays of light without showing too much detail of the moldering curtains.

By four o'clock, our nerves were stretched taut. There was nothing more to be done but prepare our own toilettes. I had some trouble finding what I wanted in my new room, for my belongings were thrown helter-skelter on the bed and chairs. At least the gowns were hanging in the clothes-press, and I went to select one. Despite my hazel eyes, Rachel has approved of my wearing light blue. It is my favorite color, and my blue silk is my favorite outfit for an elegant evening at home. It has a low neckline and is embellished with a bit of Mechlin lace and velvet ribbons. Besides a deal of trinkets, my jewelry box holds two necklaces. One is a small strand of pearls, from my grandmother, the other is an even smaller set of sapphires and diamonds. Rachel calls the stones ''chips,'' but they are so cleverly set in gold that they look larger than chips. I fastened the sapphires around my neck and stood back to admire the effect.

I brushed my hair till it shone, then arranged a wave to fall forward on the left side and scooped the rest of it up on the back of my head in the basket style. It looked well, but, to impress Aiglon, I decided it wasn't quite grand enough and hence entwined the pearl necklace amidst the basket of curls. This done, I went to Rachel for her approval. She nodded and handed me her bottle of perfume. One of the small perquisites of living with her was that I was allowed to use her perfume when we entertained or went out.

I noticed an old book sitting on her dressing table. Its title was *An Anecdotal History of Folkestone and Environs*.

"Is that the book you bought for Aiglon?" I asked, looking at it.

"I've changed my mind about giving it to him. It smells musty and the pages are all spotted," she said, and whisked it into a drawer. "What do you think of this, Rachel?"

My attention was distracted immediately by her latest theft. There, hanging from her ears and looking for all the world like monstrous diamond drops, were two pendants from the crystal chandelier lamps Willard had polished yesterday. I could only gasp in admiration of her cunning.

"Rachel, you really *are* up to all the rigs!" I laughed.

"You must make yourself a pair, too, Constance, but we shan't both wear them at the same time. Be sure you take them from the inner side of the lamps. They'll never be missed. I took mine from the lamp by the door, so you get yours from the other one."

"Aiglon will think they're diamonds and won't be so generous in future," I warned.

"Generous?" she asked, staring. "It is news to me if running this shambles of a place for one hundred pounds a year is generosity!"

"A hundred pounds! You never told me he *paid* you!" I gasped.

A pink blush suffused her face. She hadn't meant to reveal that fact, and if I had had my wits about me, I would have realized she was quite upset. In retrospect, I wonder if she carefully chose the moment of revelation to put that

18

book, which she had so swiftly shuffled into her drawer, out of my mind. I wouldn't put it past her.

"It doesn't begin to cover the expenses," Rachel said, and arose. But I knew the expense of the servants was covered separately from this salary. "We shall have a glass of wine before dinner. I hope he comes on time," she continued, dismissing the former topic. "His note said he'd be here for dinner. I daresay he will be expecting city hours, but he shan't find them here."

As we descended the stairs the view of the front hall was unusually fine after all our hard work. The old marble floor shone, and the lamps twinkled cheerfully, casting a glow on the woodwork and gilt frames. This seemed to put Rachel in a good mood.

"Perhaps we'll have *one* party while Aiglon is with us," she said. "It seems a shame not to show off our work to the community. We owe Lord Ware an invitation, and the Wigginses—any number of people."

I was already excited by the approaching visit of Aiglon. I peered hopefully into the near future and envisioned a whole new style of life, with parties and beaux. We discussed the party while awaiting Aiglon's arrival. After fifteen minutes, we had settled the guest list and menu. After half an hour, we had taken our second glass of wine and began to lose interest in the party. The talk now was of overdone meat and whipped cream that had begun to return to liquid. As the sun's rays lengthened and grew weak, Rachel more than once mentioned eating without Aiglon. She wouldn't do it, of course, but she seemed to take some satisfaction in making the threat. "I've never been so hungry in my life," she said wearily.

Then it happened. We discerned a distant thud of hooves and darted to the window. Soon a few moving dark spots— horses or carriage—showed above the thornbushes that guard the road, and before long the horses came into view. It looked and sounded like a whole herd of animals.

"Good God, I swear there weren't less than a half dozen horses pounding by the window!" Rachel squealed. "Does he expect me to stable *six* horses?"

Aiglon didn't stop at the front door but drove directly to the stable and entered the house via the kitchen. The glory of shining marble and polished chandeliers would not be his first impression of her housekeeping after all. What he would see was Meg in the kitchen surrounded by pots and pans. Rachel refused to budge until he came to her. Her nose was nearly pulled into her mouth by the time his tread was heard coming along the hall toward the saloon.

The door opened and a well-knit young gentleman, outfitted in the highest kick of fashion, glided into the room. His dark hair was carefully clipped in the stylish Brutus do. His face was lean and rather tanned, the nose well-sculpted but hawkish, giving him a predatory air. His eyes were dark, their color not distinguishable in the shadows of the saloon, but they glittered, and darted about from myself to Rachel to the window. I noticed he wore a well-cut jacket of blue Bath cloth, and at his neck was a pristine maze of intricate folds and creases that shone immaculately white. He had Rachel's knack of remaining elegant even during travel. There wasn't a wrinkle in his faun trousers, and considering the rain, his Hessians were remarkably shiny.

The apparition advanced toward me, hand extended, with a smile lifting the corners of his lips. "Cousin Rachel, delighted to see you again. How long has it been? Over a decade, I warrant. You look lovely as usual."

"I am not Rachel!" I exclaimed, mortified to have been mistaken for a forty-year-old dame.

Rachel's thin laugh floated on the air. "Pay him no heed, Constance. Aiglon is playing off one of his little jokes. He

20

is a famous jokesmith," she said, not displeased with this particular effort. "Come here and kiss your cousin, you rogue," she commanded easily.

Aiglon made a show of embarrassment and confusion, but there was a spark of mischief in those dark eyes. He bestowed a peck on Rachel's arid cheek and then returned his attention to me. "And this would be Miss Bethel," he said, extending his hand.

"Pethel," I corrected.

"Quite. A relative of Sir John, I believe?"

"Yes, he was Mama's brother."

"It is kind of you to bear Rachel company. Are you making a long visit?"

"Yes, rather. I live here," I replied.

Aiglon seated himself on the far end of my sofa, halfway between Rachel and myself.

"A glass of wine, Aiglon? Tell us all the news from London. How is your dear mama?" Rachel asked. She filled a glass of wine from the side table and handed it to him.

"She was enjoying a fit of vapors when I left."

"She should have come with you. The sea air would do her any amount of good," Rachel said.

"She prefers the smoke and fog and clamor of London. I am the one who seeks respite from it."

"And is that why you're here, to rest and take the sea air?" Rachel inquired politely. "You look stout enough to me, I must say. What is the trouble, Aiglon?"

"The lungs," he answered readily, and gave a little cough to bolster this claim to invalidism. "But I am by no means a bed-case. I've brought a few mounts to do some riding. In fact, I drove my curricle down, and my grooms are bringing my traveling carriage behind me. I hope my stable here can accommodate eight extra nags."

"*Eight!*" Rachel exclaimed in horror. "I thought it was

21

only six. I mean, six," she corrected, for she didn't wish to give the notion that even six were acceptable.

"Yes, only eight," he agreed. "But you must not think I mean to be a burden to your people. I brought my own grooms and valet and footmen to attend to my needs. I shall be very little bother to you, Cousin." He smiled blandly at the end of this awful revelation.

"How many? Grooms and footmen, I mean?" Rachel asked, her face blanching.

"Just a couple of grooms and two or three footmen. I hadn't realized Thornbury was so small, or I could have made do with one groom."

"Yes, it is very small," she told him, hinting that he might still return the excess staff to London.

His next speech showed me that Rachel had met her match. "Then I shall write to Riddell and tell him not to come. I don't want to be any trouble to you at all."

His expectant face said as clearly as words that he anticipated praise for his consideration, perhaps even a polite insistence that Riddell come by all means.

"Unless your man of business enjoys sleeping in the cellar, you had best not ask him to come" was Rachel's reply. It was delivered in faint accents. The fight had been shocked out of her for the moment.

There was a little edge returning to her voice when she continued speaking. "I don't want to rush you, Aiglon, but dinner has been waiting an age. We keep country hours here."

"Dinner? I couldn't eat a bite. I am fagged after the trip and shall retire now for the night. Perhaps a cup of broth in my room in about an hour. I could eat no more. Tomorrow I shall look forward to trying some of the local seafood."

"Just as you like, Aiglon," Rachel replied, perfectly

livid around the mouth from her efforts to control her spleen.

"Thank you so much. I don't want you to go to any special trouble for me. Will you have the servants bring me up plenty of hot water for a bath now? Oh, and there is just one other thing. I am rather a light sleeper. If you could keep the noise down tonight and in the early morning, I would appreciate it. You don't keep a rooster, I hope?"

"Of course we keep a rooster! How shall we have any increase in the henhouse without a rooster?" She was vexed into replying.

"Pity."

"You won't hear it if you keep your window closed," she said through thin lips.

"I always sleep with my window open. I came for the sea breezes." He arose languidly and sauntered toward the door. "Ah, there is just one other thing," he exclaimed, turning back to Rachel.

She stiffened in preparation for some new outrage but said nothing, and Aiglon spoke on. "I have a small favor to request. It won't cost you a penny," he added, unable to quite control some little unsteadiness of his lips. "I would prefer you not tell anyone I am here. If I am seen driving about the countryside, as I probably shall be, you might say that your cousin, Lance Howell, is visiting you for a month or so."

"A month!" she asked, staring, and forgot to be angry at the bizarre request he had made.

"More or less."

"But why do you want to use your name rather than your title?"

"Why, to tell the truth, Cousin, my visit here is a secret," he answered reasonably.

"A secret from whom?"

23

"From the law. There is a little matter of murder that I am currently involved in," he explained calmly.

"You are wanted for murder?" she asked, nonplussed, as I was myself.

"I am wanted in that regard, yes."

"Aiglon, are you brazenly standing there and telling me you killed a man in cold blood?" she asked, her voice trembling. It takes a good deal to make Rachel tremble.

"No, no, of course not. It was done in hot blood—a duel," he explained as though that were justification enough.

Then he made a graceful bow to his cousin, another to me, and sauntered out of the room and toward the stairs. Within seconds there was a loud thumping as his foot became entangled in the newly laid carpeting. A curse rent the air.

Rachel jumped up to go to his aid, and I followed her. Aiglon was pushing at the bellied carpet with his toe. "There is something amiss here," he said, frowning.

"It is newly laid—the workmen did shoddy work. I shall call them back to fix it," Rachel said hastily.

"Newly laid? But why did you have a spotty old carpet put down?" he asked. "You should have bought a new piece while you were about it."

She rushed on to distract him, no doubt relieved that he hadn't taken the time to glance at her note to Riddell. "Aiglon, about this secrecy business you mentioned. I have already told a few people you are coming. The fact will be well known in the countryside by now. You should have told me it was a secret when you wrote to me. I really think the best thing would be for you to dart on to Westleigh immediately."

"That's the first place they'll look for me," he answered. "No one knows I even own this little place. It's a pity you announced my arrival, but you can always claim

24

I didn't get here after all. If the Bow Street Runners show up, I may have to leave, but I wouldn't expect to see them for a few days yet."

As he spoke, his eyes went from her dangling pendant earrings to the lamps in the hall, comparing the design. "You will rehang those crystals when you're through with them, won't you, Cousin? I know you take excellent care of Thornbury for me. I look forward to touring the house tomorrow and seeing all the pretty new carpets and curtains and things you've had put in. And now I bid you good night once more. And you, Miss Pethel," he added, with a bow in my direction and an impish eye that told me he knew a good deal more about Rachel's housekeeping than he let on.

Rachel was struck mute. She nodded and dragged her feet slowly back to the saloon.

"Let's eat," I suggested.

Rachel plopped down on the sofa and took up her glass of wine. She looked quite dazed. "You eat, Constance. I have a little planning to do before I retire," she said.

CHAPTER THREE

I KNEW RACHEL WOULDN'T REALLY PASS UP ALL THE DEL-
icacies that we had prepared to tempt Aiglon into a good
humor. Before I had half finished my turbot, she came and
joined me at the table.

"Did you speak to the servants about Aiglon's hot water,
Rachel, or do you want me to do it?" I asked.

"I told Willard," she answered grumpily. "Hot water—
that is exactly what we are in, Constance."

"Let's enjoy this lovely dinner before we start to
worry," I suggested. "It would be a pity to waste it."

"Waste it? Fat chance of that with all of Aiglon's servants stuffing their faces belowstairs! I hope he means to
share the expenses while he is here. Eight horses! Have
you any idea how much *one* horse eats?"

"A great deal, I'm sure, but it is only hay and oats after
all," I pointed out, trying to cheer her.

"We must get rid of him, Constance, at once! Now, I
have been thinking . . ."

"I was sure you would be," I replied innocently.

"You shall see a Bow Street Runner in Folkestone tomorrow morning. He will be inquiring for Lord Aiglon.
You will make a quick dash home, and that will be the end
of him. He'll leave."

This settled, she helped herself to a plate of turbot, for the servants were all belowstairs in hands with Aiglon's bathwater, and began to eat.

"That man has eyes like a hawk," she lamented as she reached for the peas. "How did he see the grease spots on the carpet? It was dark as pitch, and the bit at the bottom of the stairs was clean. And the crystal pendants! How did he notice where they came from? Those quick eyes of his see too much. We *must* be rid of him."

Rachel has a way of accomplishing what she wants to accomplish, and I had a strong feeling that she'd get Aiglon rooted out of his own house within a day or two, but till he left life would be interesting. The first item of interest was her order to Willard to wake the rooster half an hour before usual and remove it to a spot beneath Aiglon's window. Willard was further commanded to prod it with a stick for maximum crowing. Willard agreed without so much as a question. Before she took fork to fowl, she had also told Willard to order several hundred pounds of hay and present the bill to Aiglon before he left. And, if all else failed, she meant to inundate the house with guests, since he obviously wished to be left alone.

"We shall see who is in charge here," she announced after Willard left.

I found it strange that she didn't once refer to the trifling matter of Aiglon's having killed a man. Any pleasure I had been anticipating in a flirtation with him dissipated when I learned that.

"I wonder who it is that he killed," I said during one of Rachel's respites from talking.

"Someone like him that the world is well rid of," she told me firmly.

After dinner she removed her earrings and hung them back on the lamp. We were just at the doorway doing this when the knocker sounded. As Willard was belowstairs, I

27

answered the door. Expecting to see a Bow Street Runner, Rachel wore a hopeful face, but it was only Mickey Dougherty. He came to call occasionally but seldom in the evening unless there was good reason, such as the delivery of a bottle of brandy from Madame Bieler. Rachel's purchases were rare, however, and she had just made one, so I was curious to learn why he had come.

"Why, good evening, Mickey. Come in," I said, and looked over my shoulder to tell Rachel who had arrived. I was astonished at the angry, almost frightened expression she wore.

"Good evening to you, ladies," Mickey said, making a bow. "I've just left my mount in the stable, and I see by the quantity of horseflesh there that you've got company. Lord Aiglon, is it?" he asked, darting a bold smile to Rachel.

"It is my cousin Mr. Lance Howell who is visiting," she replied stiffly. "Did you want anything in particular, Mickey, or is this a social call?" she asked. She didn't invite him into the saloon. We were usually grateful to anyone who went to the inconvenience of paying us a visit and ordinarily treated them civilly.

"I'm only here for the pleasure of seeing you. Is Aiglon traveling incognito?" Mickey asked, apparently quite aware of his lordship's family name. "That's surely odd. What could be the reason for it?"

"No special reason," she said vaguely.

I kept looking toward the saloon, mutely reminding Rachel that our guest was still standing in the hallway. Finally she relented and asked him in. I'm usually a few paces behind Rachel in my thinking, but at about that time I figured out that she meant for Mickey to spread the news of her cousin's arrival. The Wares were the likeliest people in the neighborhood to get word back to London, for Lord

Ware often went there. He was assembling statuary for his park.

"I thought maybe it had something to do with—"

"No, no, there's no special reason for his visit," she interrupted swiftly.

"I thought that, too, Mickey," I said. "I was sure his coming had something to do with Napoleon's possible invasion, but if it has, he didn't mention it. We must ask him tomorrow."

Mickey gave me a surprised look, but when he spoke, he said only, "Why don't you ask him tonight?"

"He's gone to bed," Rachel replied.

"Has he now? And who's the gentleman out walking along the beach then? He has a lordly look about him. I made sure it was Aiglon."

"A man on the beach?" I asked, and went to the window. The beach isn't actually visible from the saloon, but a man walking on the beach might take the road up to Thornbury. Our house is a little isolated from the others, and we take proprietary interest in anyone who is nearby on foot, providing he looks like a gentleman.

Indeed there was a gentleman strolling toward the house.

"It *is* Lord Aiglon!" I exclaimed, looking a question to Rachel. "What's he doing out there? He asked for hot bathwater and broth."

"He was just taking a breath of air, it looked like," Mickey said, and walked to the window. "Yes, that's the same man right enough."

I made small talk with Mickey while Rachel prepared her setdown for Aiglon. I expected Aiglon would sneak in by the back door, through which he had apparently left, but he strolled nonchalantly to the front door and let himself in.

Rachel came to attention to do battle with him. "You

shouldn't be walking outdoors right after a hot bath, Aiglon," she said.

"Aiglon?" he asked, as though he'd never heard the name before.

"He knows," Rachel replied, tossing her head toward Mickey.

"I see. Well, to put your mind at rest, Cousin, I haven't yet had my bath. There wasn't sufficient water. While my footmen prepared some, I decided to walk away the cricks and cramps of travel." He turned his attention to Mickey and continued speaking. "I don't believe I have the pleasure of your guest's acquaintance, despite his knowing who I am."

Mickey arose and pumped Aiglon's hand. He introduced himself before Rachel had the opportunity to do it for him. I poured wine for the company, and we all settled in to chat while Aiglon's water was readied.

"Is it Boney that brings you down from London?" Mickey inquired. "You're with the F.O., I believe I've heard my stepfather say."

"Bonaparte?" Aiglon asked, his fine eyebrows lifting. "No, on the contrary, I hesitated to come to the east coast at this time because of the possibility of invasion, but then I don't expect anything will come of it."

"You are quite mistaken there, Aiglon," Rachel said. "We expect to hear the roar of guns any day now." Her hope, of course, was to frighten him away.

"Surely precautions have been taken?" he said. "The military has installations on the coast, and there is the militia as well."

"I personally wouldn't expect a bunch of farmers with turnip hoes and rakes and shovels to defend me," Rachel pointed out. "We shall be in a fine pickle if the French come."

"You are too kind to worry about me," Aiglon said,

"but, in the unlikely event of an attack, I have packed my French grammar and shall introduce myself as *Monsieur Aigle*."

This pusilanimous course earned him three rebukeful stares. Mickey shook his head and said, "You're all welcome to a berth on my boat if we see the fleet coming. I can outrun anything the French have in the water. We'll nip down the channel and scoot over to the *ould* sod—Ireland."

"You're in shipping, are you, Mr. Dougherty?" Aiglon inquired with some show of interest. "Does the invasion scare interfere with your business?"

"Shipping is a bit too grand to describe what I do," Mickey answered. "What I have is a nifty three-masted lugger. I use her for fishing or a bit of short-distance hauling, and for pleasure."

"What pleasure do you find in sharing your space with a cargo of aromatic fish?" Aiglon inquired.

" 'Tis a bit of a problem," Mickey admitted readily. "But a good dose of bleach does wonders for the stench."

It was, of course, the smell of brandy that necessitated these occasional rinsings out with bleach. I believe it was another of his ploys to dump a load of bass or gray mullets on top of his real cargo. He never sold any fish but ones that liked the estuaries and those he bought from local fishermen to lend an aura of legality to what he did.

"I'll sprinkle her with attar of roses if you'd do me the honor of joining me some fine afternoon, Lord Aiglon," he added, smiling blandly.

"We shall see. My own yacht will be coming forward in a day or two." An invitation for Mickey to join Aiglon was not offered, but Mickey took no offense. He was really the best-natured man in the county.

There was a little more general conversation, after which Mickey said, "I wonder if I might have a word with you in private, Lady Savage? Business,'' he added for Aiglon's and my benefit.

"Certainly. We'll go to the study. Excuse us, Aiglon.''

They left, and Aiglon smiled at me. I was extremely uncomfortable at being abandoned to the sole company of a murderer and sought for any excuse to escape. "I'll see if your bathwater is ready yet," I said, and arose.

"No, stay," he said, rather imperiously. I sat down again and waited to hear what he had to say.

"What business would Mr. Dougherty have with my cousin?" he asked.

"I don't know. He doesn't usually have any business with her. I was quite curious myself.''

"Surely her fishmonger doesn't visit her to be entertained in her saloon?" he prodded.

"Good gracious, no! Mickey's not a fishmonger. He's a smuggler, but Rachel bought a bottle just a day ago, so it can't be that. He might have a new load of silk he's telling her about. She usually gets it directly from Madame Bieler. That's who handles the silk and small orders of brandy for Mickey," I explained.

All this is as well known as a ballad in our area, so I was surprised when Aiglon broke out into a sardonic laugh at hearing it.

"It's comforting to know I have such law-abiding citizens keeping house for me," he said.

"At least we haven't murdered anyone!" I shot back.

He leaned forward and smiled softly. "I may have overstated the case. I hit my man, but whether it was a fatal shot is not certain. I felt it wise to leave before the doctor was called," he explained.

"Who did you shoot?"

"A Mr. Kirkwell.''

"Why did you do it?" I stared in fascination. I had never seen a murderer before, and wasn't likely to do so

32

again, but somehow I never thought a murderer would look as refined and civilized as Aiglon.

"Because I was drunk," he answered bluntly. There was no air of apology in the speech though perhaps a little embarrassment.

"But you must have had time to sober up between the challenge and the duel. There is the business of seconds and of arranging a meeting place . . ."

"I was drunk for two days," he assured me.

He didn't look as dissipated as all that. Men who are habitually drunk have ravaged faces and bleary eyes. Aiglon had about the sharpest pair of eyes I had ever encountered, and his flesh was firm.

"I hope this has taught you a lesson," I said, and looked at the study door. Rachel had closed it behind her. I wished she would finish her business with Mickey and return, for I could think of nothing more to say to Lord Aiglon.

"Yes, I see that it was a mistake," he admitted. "I came to Thornbury to get away from the sort of company I have fallen into recently. Here in the peace and quiet of the countryside, I hope to convert myself to a more proper course."

I looked at him suspiciously, but there was no smile, no mischief luring in those dark eyes now. He seemed perfectly sincere. My feelings for Aiglon pulled me two ways. Since my closest friend was so very anxious to be rid of him, I half wanted him gone, too, but I was Christian enough to wish to help a man who seeks the road to reformation. I glanced at the wineglass on the table. He'd had two or three refills since he'd arrived. I must warn Rachel to put the decanters away.

"I know what you're thinking," he said in a low voice. "But one or two social drinks will do me no harm. I can manage that with perfect ease so long as I am in the proper company. I think you will be very proper company, Miss Pethel.''

The only handsome man who had ever looked at me in such a way was Mickey Dougherty, and he looked at every other woman in the countryside the same way. In fact, his expression wasn't much different when conversing with his horse. Aiglon's was a soft, admiring, hopeful look, which sent my imagination soaring.

What wonderful miracle had occurred here? How had providence been so kind as to drop an enormously eligible gentleman into the wilds of Thornbury, where there wasn't a maiden for miles except me? The discrepancy between our material states was mitigated by his liquor problem. He was a lord, and I was a lady of small means, but at least I was a lady. More highly born families might have been reluctant to involve their daughters with a man who drank too much, but not my family. Besides, I could cure him of that. He had the desire to be cured, and that was half the battle. His having killed a man was a great hurdle, of course. But then it wasn't certain Aiglon *had* killed him, and, even if he had, it wasn't a planned cold-blooded murder. In any case, Aiglon would be an interesting addition to our household. I now had the desire to keep him at Thornbury, and the large problem of talking Rachel around to my view.

Just when I was beginning to feel at ease with Aiglon, the study door opened and Rachel and Mickey came out, wreathed in smiles. Whatever little antagonism had existed between them had been cleared up. ''She must have struck a good bargain on the silk,'' Aiglon said to me in a low tone, and smiled as though we were conspirators. It was a warm, intimate smile.

Mickey took up a seat and settled in comfortably with a fresh glass of wine. Aiglon turned to him and said, ''Perhaps you could help me find a good safe berth for my yacht, Mr. Dougherty. I was looking along the waterfront here, and I notice there are no docking facilities."

"The harbor at Folkestone is the place you want, Lord Aiglon. I'll have my lads keep an eye on it for you. Or will you be bringing crew of your own?"

Rachel looked alarmed, but Aiglon's reply calmed her down. "I have a three-man crew who will sleep aboard. You must come out with me one day and tell me what you think of the Mermaid."

"Is that what you call her? I'll look forward to it. Why, between your *Mermaid* and my old vessel, we won't have a thing to fear from Boney," Mickey said. "You can put away your French grammar and rest easy."

"I don't actually have a French grammar with me." Aiglon smiled. "I'm part French myself, you know. The strain goes back to Norman times but has been frequently refurbished by French brides since that age. I'm not one of those Englishmen who has an innate hatred or mistrust of the French. I expect that an Irishman like you feels some affinity with them as well."

"Ah, no, I'm not one of the Papist Irish. There's plenty in the old country who laugh up their sleeves at England's troubles at this time, but I'm on the right side, as you might say," Mickey explained. "I'm in the militia and all. You'll have to come out and see us practice one of these evenings, milord."

"The waltz of the turnip hoes and spades?" Aiglon smiled. "Isn't it possible to get guns for the militia? I should think the army would supply them at such a crucial time as this, Mr. Dougherty."

"Call me Mickey. Everyone does. There're plenty of us who have guns. The army was supposed to distribute Brown Besses two weeks ago, but nothing came of it. You might know something about that, Lord Aiglon, since you're hot from London." He looked expectantly for an answer.

"I'm afraid that's not my area of interest. I'm involved in the Peninsular campaign," Aiglon replied.

"Still, you have the ear of the lads in London. Anything you could do in the way of getting us some arms would be appreciated. It'd do morale a deal of good. When the men are not decently armed, spirits *do* flag."

I was disappointed at Aiglon's lack of interest. "I should think your best bet would be to apply to Colonel Denby," he said in a rather bored way. He displayed such little interest in the subject that I was surprised he even knew that Denby was in charge of the local supply.

"We've applied to Denby more than once," Mickey replied, but he saw Aiglon's lack of interest and dropped the subject.

Willard came clomping in and informed Lord Aiglon that his bath was ready, and the two men made indefinite plans to meet again soon. When Aiglon left, Mickey, with his spirits unimpaired, also took his leave. Rachel and I were left alone.

"Rachel," I said at once, "did you know Aiglon was dead drunk when he shot that man? He drinks a good deal. I think we should get the decanter out of his room."

"All the Howells are good drinkers. He's been bamming you, Constance. How could he hit his man if he were drunk?"

I was taken back by Rachel's logic. She continued speaking while I pondered the point. "The Howells are also notorious womanizers. I shouldn't have thought you were Aiglon's type, but then you're prettier than either Meg or I, and that doesn't leave him a great deal of choice. A word to the wise, Constance. Don't trust him.''

I blushed for my foolish vanity. "You're right, of course. As usual." But after considering the situation a moment longer, I added, "It could have been a lucky shot—I mean, it could be an accident that Aiglon hit his man."

"Yes, and the moon could be made of blue cheese, for all we know, but one is wiser to assume that the probable is what did, in fact, occur."

We sat a moment in silence. "Aiglon says he came here to get away from the companions he usually drinks with. It would be wrong to hasten him away if he really wants to reform."

"I can't believe my ears!" Rachel exclaimed, casting a look of scorn at me. "Constance, if that rake has bothered to bring you under his thumb, he can only mean to make some improper use of you. I leave it to your imagination to figure out what use that might be. I am more determined than ever to get rid of him. Now I must go and speak to Willard. We'll have to arrange some diversion for Aiglon tomorrow morning so that he forgets a tour of the house. You will proceed to Folkestone, as planned, and return with word that the place is swarming with Runners looking for Aiglon. For a start, I must remind Willard not to wake the rooster early. The longer that troublesome wretch stays in bed, the better."

With those angry words she arose and went after Willard. Remembering the state my room was in, I decided to put it in order and went upstairs. Aiglon's room was across the hall and down from mine. His door was open and as I passed I saw him in conversation with his valet, a dapper little man with curly brown hair and a sharp nose. There was a large copper tub full of water on the floor, but Aiglon ignored it. He was fully dressed, by which I mean not only that he wasn't preparing for his bath, but that he had actually donned a greatcoat and curled beaver. He was going out, and there wasn't a doubt in my mind that he was headed for the closest tavern.

So much for his wish for reformation!

CHAPTER FOUR

THE DAY HAD BEEN HARROWING ENOUGH THAT I SLEPT despite knowing Aiglon was out drinking. What had it to do with me if a young gentleman with every advantage should decide to ruin himself with drink? Running away from his London companions may have been well intentioned, but he'd have no trouble finding new drinking companions in Folkestone. He'd already made the acquaintance of one of the best topers in the area: Mickey Dougherty. In fact, it came to my mind that Aiglon's cool attitude toward Mickey had warmed when he learned that Mickey was a smuggler. He didn't want to meet reputable people, but he hadn't been slow to offer a brandy smuggler a sail on his yacht.

I was in a disgruntled frame of mind when I went downstairs to breakfast. Rachel was already there, frowning into her gammon and eggs.

"I hope Willard didn't kill the rooster, in an excess of zeal," she said. "I haven't heard a peep out of him this morning. At least it's kept Aiglon in bed till a decent hour."

"What has kept your cousin abed is not the silence from chanticleer, Rachel. He was out till all hours last night."

She looked positively stricken. "No! You don't mean he was out snooping around already!"

"Snooping around for what? He wasn't looking for remains of the dovecote by the light of the moon. He was out *drinking*," I told her.

This called for an explanation of what I had seen on my way to bed. "That sounds like him, right enough," she answered mildly. She appeared quite satisfied with his behavior, perhaps because it showed me what he was really like. "We shall proceed with our plan. You'll be leaving for Folkestone right after breakfast?"

"It's only eight o'clock!"

"There's no rush then. You'll have time to speak to Cook and see what she needs for dinner. Aiglon has asked that we go to no pains on his behalf, and I mean to take him at his word. I shall serve fish stew and bread pudding," she announced grimly.

Cook makes the worst fish stew in the world. It has nothing in common with the French dish. It consists of cod or plaice boiled with onions in milk and thickened with flour.

"Excellent. He mentioned wanting to try the local seafood," I said.

No sooner had these words left my mouth than we heard Aiglon's footsteps approaching. He bowed into the room, inquiring most civilly how we had slept.

"I slept like a babe," he told us, and his bright eyes did not belie it. "I foresee that a prolonged visit here at Thornbury will do me any amount of good. Have you any plans for the day, Cousin?"

"My day is always entirely filled taking care of Thornbury," she replied stiffly.

"Indeed? I shouldn't have thought running a little cottage would even begin to tap your resources, Rachel. And you, Miss Pethel? Is your time all occupied in the same manner?"

"Miss Pethel is going into town for me this morning," Rachel told him.

"Excellent. I shall accompany her," he said, and helped himself to the gammon while I looked at Rachel for instructions.

She nodded her head ever so slightly, but enough to inform an old accomplice like me that she consented. It would stave off Aiglon's tour of Thornbury, of course, and give her an extra morning to rearrange the tatters of draperies and canopies. What it would not do, however, is permit me to let on that I had seen a swarm of Runners.

After we had all breakfasted and I went for my pelisse, Rachel came to my room. "I'll have to receive word of the Runners' arrival after lunch," she said. "Keep him away as long as you can." She gave me the shopping list, casually mentioning that if Aiglon wished to pay cash instead of putting the purchases on her account, I should not demur. In that unlikely case, I was to purchase many more items than were on the list.

It was about nine o'clock when I finally went downstairs ready for the trip. I was very interested to be handed up into Aiglon's sporting curricle, which was drawn by a team of prize grays, and very ill at ease when I saw how low were the edges of the seat that were to hold us in place. Aiglon snapped the whip above the horses' heads, and they took off at a speed that whipped my neck back quite painfully and knocked my bonnet askew.

We rattled along at a pace that precluded conversation till we came to the tents where the regiment was stationed. We stopped a few minutes to watch the men drilling. "Will you drive in and speak to Colonel Denby?" I asked.

"Perhaps another time. I have a rather urgent errand in town," he answered, and drove on.

41

I was at a loss to know what his errand might be, for when we reached town he turned to the Leas, where he wasn't likely to meet anyone but tourists or citizens out taking the air. I gave some hint of my thinking, and he reined in.

"Why, to tell the truth, my errand is here with Mother Nature," he said playfully, and inhaled a deep breath of sea air.

"That, I believe, is the same truth you were purveying last night when you said you were going to take a bath?" I asked, and subjected him to a sharp stare.

"But I did bathe!"

"Did you? Is it the fashion in London to don a coat and hat for the purpose? How practical. It takes care of the laundry at the same time!"

"I hadn't realized I was an object of such interest that my every move was monitored," he said, turning his head and smiling in what he no doubt considered an irresistible manner. It was the same warmly intimate smile he had offered the previous evening in the saloon. "Tell me, Miss Pethel, did Foote leave the door ajar, or did you peek in the keyhole?"

I did not honor this question with a reply. "I was merely surprised to see you dressed for outdoors when I went to my room. Did you find a congenial drinking partner, Lord Aiglon?"

"Is this the face of a man who was drinking last night?" he asked, leaning toward me till his youthful visage nearly touched mine. And certainly it bore no signs of ravage.

"What were you doing then?" I asked, pulling back.

"Wine is not the only dissipation that mortal flesh is heir to. Use your imagination, ma'am."

"But you just got here yesterday! You couldn't have found a woman already!" I exclaimed.

His bright eyes opened wider. He set his head back and

laughed so loudly that several people turned in our direction. "True enough," he answered, "that will take another day. But I did find an unexceptionable inn, where a few gentlemen were kind enough to invite me to join a game of cards. And before you scold me about drinking while playing, let me inform you I had only two small beers the whole evening."

I felt rather foolish and, in lieu of apologizing, attacked on a new front. "I suppose you lost a great deal of money?"

"On the contrary, I made six shillings. Etiquette decrees that I give the gentlemen the opportunity to recoup their losses within a day or two. So if you happen to see an empty bed next time your eye finds itself at my keyhole, you'll know where I am."

"I didn't peek in the keyhole."

He cocked his head to one side and examined me for a moment. "It must have been Rachel. I didn't think you were the keyhole sort, but one never knows. You are at least an accessory to her other crimes."

"I'm just a guest at Thornbury. How she keeps house for you is no affair of mine," I said airily.

He wagged a shapely finger under my nose. "Faint-hearted, Miss Pethel. I expected more fire from you. I have it on the best authority, namely the kitchen help, that you, with your own lily-whites, wielded the hammer that installed that spotted rag on the front stairs. I stick by the word 'accessory.' How came you to make your home here? Are you an orphan?" he asked, settling into a less playful mood.

"Not at all. I have a full set of parents along with several brothers and sisters."

"Enough of these brothers and sisters that your going was not a tragedy?" he asked.

"If you are politely trying to gauge my social back-

43

ground, Lord Aiglon, you have hit the nail on the head. Papa was sorry but not reluctant to see one of us bounced off, to make room for the rest. I am the eldest and hence I seemed the logical one to leave when the invitation came from Lady Savage.''

''But surely, even if the dowry is small or, indeed, non-existent, are not attractive young ladies more usually bounced off to the tune of wedding bells?''

''At the time it was thought that I might meet someone here,'' I admitted. If there is a woman in the world strong enough to make such an utterance without blushing, I have yet to meet her. ''I didn't have any particular beau in Kent.''

''What a slow bunch of tops! And *have* you met someone here?''

''No, I haven't.''

''What a slow top *you* are, too! I shall find you a *parti* before I leave. I hereby make a solemn promise, Miss Constance Pethel, that you won't be required to return home hanging your head in shame.''

''What a strange thing to say!''

His brows lifted and a rather diabolical smile settled upon his face. ''You must have noticed by now that I'm rather a strange, impetuous man,'' he answered, then whipped the horses into motion and drove down into the village.

Rachel's plan of getting him to pay for the shopping was nipped in the bud. He left me the minute we arrived and went his own way, arranging to meet me at the hotel in an hour. I saw him twice during the intervening hour. In one instance he was going into the real estate office—for what reason I couldn't imagine, unless Mr. Roundtree, the agent, was one of his gambling buddies. The other time he was talking to Mickey outside of the "everything" store. We met at ten-thirty, as planned.

"Are you in a hurry to get home?" he asked.

"Not particularly, but I don't wish to delay my package too long. Fish," I explained, handing it to him to stow in the curricle.

"This won't take long. I was chatting to Mickey, and he invited me over to the headquarters of the militia to meet the officer and discuss their preparations."

The drills were executed at the east end of the Leas. The headquarters consisted of a little room at the back of the Church of St. Mary and St. Eanswith, which is situated there. The church was heavily involved in the whole defense, and the minister kept watch for bonfires that would send him to ring the bells. The officer was Captain Cokewell, a retired army man. We were considered fortunate to have a real military man in charge of the militia.

We drove directly along to the church, and I saw Mickey's fine bay mare tethered outside. As we drove up, Mickey and Captain Cokewell came out to greet us. Mickey made the introduction, and Cokewell invited Aiglon in to have a look at his maps and plan of strategy. The defenses were rather pathetic, really—just the furze stacks, men to keep an eye on the coast, and, of course, the local merchants and farmers, who would defend their land with cabbage stumps and hurdle sticks or whatever ancient weapons they possessed. Cokewell realized these inadequacies and urged Aiglon to speak to the powers in London about getting real weapons, while I sat silently on a chair in the corner.

Cokewell wore a moustache and whiskers and possessed a loud, military sort of voice. "We've been promised weapons for months," he told Aiglon.

Aiglon rubbed his forehead, perplexed. "I seem to remember hearing that weapons were on their way to this area some time ago. Did the army preempt them?" he asked.

"Devil a bit of it. They never reached the area at all," Cokewell said. "The load was coming by sea from Bristol and was pirated. The ship had put in at the Isle of Wight for the night, and no one worried about it. The captain gave his lads the night off, leaving a few guards aboard, of course. The bunch of them got drunk and the guns vanished. I'll tell you this much, milord, they never showed up in *England*," he said. His wise face said as clearly as words that the guns had been spirited across the Channel to France.

"I heard nothing about that in London!" Aiglon exclaimed, horrified.

"You wouldn't have, would you? The navy put a cap on the story to save their faces. We've been trying to get another shipment ever since. Sending them by land is the safer way. The Frenchies don't dare come right into England."

"What makes you think it was the Frenchies who took the load from the Isle of Wight?" Aiglon asked. "Without an English informer how could they even have known it was there?"

"It would be the smugglers who tipped them off," Cokewell answered unthinkingly. Mickey made a little coughing sound. "I don't mean *you*, Dougherty, obviously," Cokewell added. "Your loyalty is not in question. I don't know what I'd do without this lad," he added to Aiglon, while clapping Mickey on the shoulder in a fatherly way. "He's the best militiaman we have. Some evening you must come out to see his troop parade."

"You might use your connections to discover who *did* tip the French," Aiglon suggested to Mickey.

"Assuming I knew anything about it at all—which I don't—it could cost a man's life to squeal on the Gentlemen," Mickey exclaimed. "They operate by gangs, you see, so it'd be the Wight gang that handled the job. Not

46

the Folkestone gang. The last person who'd ever hear anything is a member of another gang."

"Still, it seems more probable to me that it was a member of the Folkestone gang who knew the arms were on their way," Aiglon suggested. "The Channel is full of ships. How did they know that particular one held arms?"

"They've ways of knowing," Mickey answered unhelpfully. "The fact of the matter is, the Gentlemen are the first ones to have the finger pointed at them. Any number of people knew about that cargo. The lads in London who ordered it in the first place, the navy, every man on the ship, and, likely as not, the officials in Wight knew, too. But it's the poor old Gentlemen who take the blame for it all."

"There's something in what Mickey says," Cokewell defended. "In any case, land is a safer means of transportation for the next load."

"If there *is* a next load," Aiglon added doubtfully.

"If there isn't, then the fall of England is on the heads of the powers at Whitehall. And on the head of any gentleman who doesn't do everything in his power to get us those weapons," Cokehall said stiffly, whiskers twitching indignantly at his unhelpful caller.

Aiglon's eyes turned to the far wall, where a pathetic collection of rusty blunderbusses and assorted sticks and poles rested to defend England. "I see your point," he replied. He didn't make any promises, but by that mute code of the English gentleman it seemed to be understood that Aiglon would bestir himself to do what he could.

Cokewell offered us wine. Aiglon declined, and we left. Mickey walked out with us. "How is Lady Savage this morning, Constance, my flower?" he asked.

"Not much changed from last night," I told him.

He turned his attention to Aiglon. "How long do you think it will take before we're armed?" he asked.

"I shall do what I can. Speed, I assume, is of the essence."

"The sooner the better. We're expecting company to land on the first night of calm sea and heavy fog. It'll be a grand fight, Aiglon. Tell me the truth now. Didn't you come clattering down here for no other purpose than to be in on it? *I* wouldn't miss it for all the poteen in Ireland!"

I considered this a grave misreading of Aiglon's character, but when I looked at him the expression in his dark eyes did not differ much from Mickey's own. It was a dancing, anticipatory, delighted look. "One *does* get tired of shuffling papers," he admitted.

"I think you're *both* insane!" I exclaimed.

"Come along, Constance, my flower," Aiglon said, and put his hand on my elbow, with a parting nod to Mickey.

It is one thing to be called "Constance, my flower" by Mickey, who calls Rachel "darling." It was quite a different experience to hear those intimate words on Aiglon's noble lips. I was quite simply astonished. As we walked away, Mickey called after us. "I should warn you, Aiglon, it's a wildflower I meant."

Aiglon looked back, a smile lighting his face. He looked from Mickey to me, as though figuring out what species I might belong to. "She's no tame blossom. I've learned that much already."

This was the most arrant nonsense. I hadn't yet done a thing to reveal a wild streak. This was some kind of masculine competition, each pretending that he knew me better than the other. I might have been as ugly as a frog and it wouldn't have mattered.

"A wild rose with thorns," Aiglon said as we went to the carriage. I believe that he was feeling a little foolish, now that we had gotten away from Mickey and he was left to face me alone.

I felt more like a climbing rose as I attempted to vault

into the curricle. Then we were off in a fine rattling of harnesses and whinnying of eager horseflesh.

"Did you conclude your business successfully?" I asked, determined to keep a polite tone.

"Quite."

"Mr. Roundtree is available for gambling this evening then, is he?"

"Gambling? No, no, it was Mickey and some friends of his I met last night. As you've been spying on me again, let me put your mind at rest. I went to see Roundtree about selling Thornbury."

This horrendous announcement was uttered without a blink. "Selling Thornbury!" I gasped. "But what about Rachel?"

"She is forever complaining about it. She'll be delighted to be relieved of the onerous chore," he said.

"But where will she go?"

"I have no idea. But I'll tell you where she will *not* go and that is to Westleigh."

As my senses stopped reeling, I rallied to Rachel's cause. "No, she would be much happier in your London residence," I answered calmly.

Aiglon's dark head turned slowly in my direction. His brow was cloudy, and the words he uttered then are not for this polite document.

CHAPTER FIVE

I WENT TEARING INTO THE HOUSE THE MINUTE AIGLON brought the curricle to a stop. Rachel was not to be found in any of her regular spots, so in desperation I ran down to the kitchen. There I found her rinsing her hands, apparently after a spell of gardening.

"I must speak to you at once, Rachel!"

"Don't tell me you couldn't find any fresh fish in town," she replied, a frown of vexation creasing her brow.

"In the study, the instant you're free," I insisted, and rushed back upstairs to store my pelisse and bonnet. It wasn't long till she joined me.

"Where is Aiglon?" she asked.

"I don't know—at the stable, I think. Rachel, Aiglon's been to a real estate agent and has put Thornbury up for sale!"

A strangled "Aaagh!" came from deep within her throat. "What did he say? What is the reason? He can't sell it now. It's impossible!"

There was a very gentle tap at the door, and Aiglon himself sauntered in, holding the packet of fish. He held it away from his body, as the wrapping had become soggy. "You forgot this in the carriage," he said, handing the

50

parcel to me. I put it aside on a table and turned to observe the cousins' exchange.

"Aiglon, you can't be serious!" Rachel charged, her eyes flashing.

"I'm afraid it's true," he answered mildly. "Miss Pethel did indeed desert the carriage and leave her important parcel behind."

"Don't be ridiculous! You know we're not talking about codfish," Rachel answered angrily.

"Cod?" he asked with a disillusioned eye at the soggy parcel. "I was hoping for shellfish."

"Is it true you're selling Thornbury?" she demanded.

"It is certainly true I have put it on the market. Whether it finds a taker is, of course, another matter."

"But why?"

"Because it is nothing but an expense to me. This is the first time I have ever set foot in the place, and I daresay it will be the last. It's poor economics to carry a place that gobbles up money for maintenance yet produces nothing."

"But it's such a charming old home, and has been in the family forever," Rachel pointed out, gliding swiftly past the shoals of maintenance monies expended.

"I happen to be dipped at the moment," Aiglon replied, and looked out the window, already bored with the conversation.

"How can you possibly be dipped? You get ten-thousand a year from Westleigh, to say nothing of—"

His head turned from the window. "I wouldn't dream of burdening you with the details of the sordid tale," he said blandly. "Suffice it to say, I need some cash rather urgently, and Thornbury is the item I am most willing to part with. I can give you a few weeks to clear out, Cousin."

"A few weeks," she said pensively.

51

"I shouldn't think I'd find a buyer who wants occupancy before that time."

"If it's just a temporary shortage, Aiglon, why don't you mortgage the place?" she suggested.

"Because mortgages have to be repaid. When an estate produces nothing but bills, it makes no sense to hold on to it," he explained patiently.

She took a deep breath and asked, "How much are you asking?"

"Roundtree suggested two thousand guineas. Does that sound a fair price to you, Cousin?"

"Two thousand guineas for this crumbling heap?" she asked, and laughed merrily but unconvincingly. "You'll be fortunate to get one thousand."

"Now *that's* odd!" Aiglon said. "Roundtree first suggested twenty-five hundred, but when he realized I was interested in a quick sale, he knocked it down to two thousand."

I realized then what Rachel was up to. She meant to buy Thornbury herself! This surprised me as she never had a good word to say for it. She had occasionally mentioned removing to Bath or even to a small flat in London, but buying Thornbury and settling down there to grow old . . . No, I must have misunderstood her thinking.

"The man is a lunatic," she declared roundly. "There is no land to speak of, and the whole place is blasted with antiquity."

"But the seaside location is attractive," he pointed out. "The house has historical associations as well. It was a Royalist rallying place when Cromwell and his firebrands were kindling strife."

"No one cares about that sort of thing nowadays," she told him.

"I must disagree with you. There are hundreds, perhaps thousands, of historical-minded people in the kingdom who

52

would be delighted to inhabit an old home such as this. Important battles were fought here in Cromwell's time. Thornbury boasts the remains of a chapel somewhere on the grounds, too."

"Yes, if you can find the chapel under the rubble," she riposted sharply. "It would cost a fortune to bring the place into livable condition."

"How can you say that, Cousin, after the fine and expensive job you have done keeping everything shipshape?" he asked, his eye sparking a challenge.

"You may count yourself fortunate if you get fifteen hundred for the place," she countered.

"We shall see. Roundtree thinks two thousand is a modest asking price, in any case. We can always go lower if we find no takers. In the meanwhile, you can begin making other plans for yourself, Cousin." He smiled pleasantly and strode from the room.

"That's the thanks I get for ten years of faithful service!" Rachel said when he had gone. "All I have to say is it serves him right."

"What serves him right?"

She looked surprised but soon answered, "Why, the fact that he has his pockets to let. I don't see how it can be possible. He must have lost a *fortune* in gambling."

She took the parcel of fish and walked out the door. I went upstairs. Aiglon's gambling in London was apparently not of the innocent kind indulged in here on the coast. It would take many nights of losing a few shillings to bankrupt a man who had ten thousand a year to play with.

Lunch was a hostile meal, the conversation consisting mainly of requests for mustard or butter and an occasional sharp word from Rachel to the footman. She didn't tell me what she meant to do after lunch, and, given her current mood, I didn't ask. I just slipped out quietly for a stroll around the estate. Though Thornbury was spoken of as having no land, it did actually include a few acres. The gardens didn't flourish, nor were they well-tended, but behind the home garden there was a tangle of growth with a rambling walk that was pretty in spring. I went there to lose myself for an hour and think about the future. If Thornbury was to be sold, then it wasn't only Rachel who had to find a new home. I too would be dispossessed, but my original home still remained, and my family would willingly take me back.

At the back of the tangled growth that was once a garden, and which still brought forth roses and other blossoms in season, was the ruined chapel. From the rubble that remained it was impossible to discern its former style. No wall rose high enough to show the original shape of the windows, but I remembered seeing in the Thornbury library old drawings of a pretty Gothic building with lancet windows of stained glass. It was called Our Lady's Chapel in those days, the lady being the Virgin Mary. I sat on a pile of stones and stared into the bush, where pretty primroses peeped above the unclipped yew hedge.

Five years of my life were about to come to an end, and I didn't know whether I was glad or sorry. I did feel, though, that it was time for a change. I had come here at age seventeen and spent my best years in this quiet backwater. I had no talent for anything but homemaking, and the obvious future for me involved a husband. Thornbury had not proved fruitful in that regard, whereas my sister Prissy had found herself an excellent *parti* at home. Mr. Thomas must have friends and relatives, some of whom were single and seeking a wife. How strange to think of little Prissy as a bride. Of course, "little Prissy" was now one and twenty.

Completely absorbed in my thoughts, I didn't hear the sound of footsteps till Aiglon was nearly beside me. I looked up and saw him just standing there, quietly gazing at me. He wore a thoughtful expression. Suddenly he raised his hand and waved a white handkerchief.

"I come in peace," he said, and walked forward. "Are you angry with me, too, Constance?"

His was a face that not even full sunlight objected to. The glancing rays picked out no incipient wrinkles, no bleariness of eye, no sagging of chin. He was in the pink of manhood. He could pose as a symbol of all that is best in England's men. Yet he was a full-fledged scoundrel who had run through a fortune, fought a duel and probably killed a man, and regularly drank himself into a stupor.

"No, not angry," I answered reluctantly. He didn't mean enough to me that I had the right to be angry, though I was certainly disillusioned. "Where's Rachel?"

"She's gone into town."

"Oh, I wish she'd told me."

"Why? You were there this morning. Did you forget something?"

"No, it's just that driving into town is our chief diversion. We usually go together." Perhaps she meant to find some imaginary Bow Street Runners. But it didn't matter much now. The catastrophe of his having put Thornbury up for sale overshadowed everything else.

"That sounds fairly tedious. Why don't we ride instead?"

"I don't have a mount."

"Mine are here. I brought two. It seems like fate, does it not?" he suggested.

"Did you also bring a lady's riding habit?"

"Ah, no! Fate slipped up there. Do you not ride then?"

"Not since coming to Thornbury. I used to ride at home."

"But since coming to this place, you only drive. Have you ever driven a curricle?"

"Driven one? I never even rode in one in all my life till this morning."

"Come along, I'll give you a lesson," he offered.

I could see that he was finding time heavy on his hands, and I resented the variety of pleasures he customarily enjoyed. "No, really, I would rather not. I've only driven one horse at a time, and not such a lively stepper as yours, Lord Aiglon."

He considered talking me out of my reluctance but changed his mind. I could read the thoughts on his mobile face and in his eyes. "Very well, then, *you* decide how we shall spend this lovely afternoon."

"There's nothing to do here, Lord Aiglon. This is how we spend our afternoons."

"Sitting on a pile of rocks, smiling at grief?" he asked, astonished at such a dull pastime. "They named you after the wrong virtue. You should have been called Patience. Or even Resignation," he added. There was a trail of taunting in his voice now.

"Two virtues that are alien to you!" I answered swiftly.

"You *are* mad at me," he replied in a wheedling tone. "You shouldn't be, Constance. You, of all people, know what a trimming Rachel has given me all these years. I didn't mind letting her have Thornbury, or even supplying money to keep it habitable for her, but for her to be lying to me—stealing is not too strong a word for it!—is the outside of enough."

As there was no defense I could mount to this charge, I sat silently while selecting a fresh offensive. "You would have preferred to fritter away the money on gambling instead, no doubt."

"At least I have a fighting chance at cards or horseracing. Only women take advantage of men," he informed me.

"The *whole world* takes advantage of women! Why were

all the estates left to *you*? Rachel was as close a relative to John Howell as you were, but Thornbury was given to you, who already had Westleigh and I don't know what all else. It is my understanding that the head of the family is to take care of the less fortunate.''

''I *do* take care of the less fortunate. But Rachel is not among them. Sir John left her pretty well-off, you know. How else do you think she's planning to buy Thornbury?''

''Do you think that's what she's up to?'' I asked, interested to hear that he shared my view.

''I don't see why else its value was suddenly cut in half.'' After this speech, Aiglon sat down beside me on the pile of rocks. ''I wonder why she doesn't want to leave. She used to be a very sociable kind of woman. Actually, I had almost decided to offer her the use of a flat in London. I recently bought a large house in Upper Grosvenor Square and had it made into four rather nice flats. I have assorted genuinely less-fortunate relatives to occupy them. The one I have in mind for Rachel is also large enough to house you, Constance.''

I ignored this show of generosity and honed in on another point. '' 'Recently'? How did you come to purchase a large house when you were dipped?'' I asked.

''The purchase is recent; my unfortunate state of poverty is *more* recent. A temporary thing only, till next quarter day,'' he added vaguely. ''And the temporary shortage is not due to gambling. It happens I invested rather heavily in lumber from Canada. I lost two ships. I may be unlucky; I hope you don't take me for a scoundrel.''

I hadn't really expected an explanation and certainly not one couched in such humble phrases. Having been somewhat encroaching in my own queries, I was embarrassed. ''You don't have to explain your affairs to me,'' I said. My voice was curt, which was not how I meant it to sound at all.

He turned a sharp, accusing eye on me. "Do I not? I had the distinct impression you were more than a little interested."

"Just curious. We haven't much to do here and perhaps I take an overweening interest in other people's affairs."

He accepted this extremely oblique apology in good spirits. "Not much to do? You are unimaginative! What is there to do elsewhere that can't be done here? You've roads for riding and driving, interesting towns and places to visit, other estates for balls and parties, the opposite sex to flirt with, and, on top of it all, the ocean at your doorstep. No, Constance, you're manufacturing some sorry bricks here without straw. The fact is you're a complete sloth who likes to do nothing better than sit on a rock and look at a garden. And a garden, incidentally, that could occupy a good deal of a woman's time had she any taste for activity."

"Perhaps you're right," I admitted. "But it *is* pleasant here in the garden, is it not?"

"The jungle is pretty, but I would have thought a confirmed sitter like yourself would have at least installed more comfortable chairs. Show me around the place," he said, arising and offering me his hand.

As the jungle was impenetrable except for the walk, I showed him the ruined chapel instead. "This used to be called Our Lady's Chapel before it was destroyed by Cromwell's men," I explained. "If you look carefully at the remaining bits of wall, you can see where the rocks were scorched by fire."

"It would be fun to rebuild it," he said. "I wonder how large it was."

He clambered through the bottom portion of a window hole and stood on the rocks below, holding his hand up to me. "Come on, let's explore. We'll see if anything interesting remains."

"There's nothing but rubble. I've explored it a dozen times," I objected, but the hand only beckoned peremptorily till I put mine in it and I was aided through the opening. Our footing was uncertain, and Aiglon kept hold of my hand to keep our balance. Or at least I expect that was his excuse. He *was* the sort of gentleman who liked women, I thought.

Most of the rocks were piled at one side of the excavation. At the other side grass grew up between the stones. "I wonder why the rocks were all removed to the east side," he said, looking around.

"Some ancestor probably planned to use them for something but lost his enthusiasm midway in the project," I suggested.

"They would make an excellent dovecote" was all he said, but his laughing eyes spoke volumes. "It was a fairly large chapel, wasn't it?" he asked, walking over to the grassy area. Our footing wasn't the least precarious here, yet still he held my hand. "In Norman times, of course, Thornbury was quite a grand residence—the original home of the Aiglon family," he explained.

"I didn't know that!"

"Oh, yes. That's why it was left to me, the present head of the house. Old John Howell had nothing against Rachel. The place traditionally has gone to Lord Aiglon."

"Then why are you selling it?" I asked.

I received a frustrated glare. He hadn't meant to tell me the house had any particular significance. "It's a case of necessity. I'm very reluctant to part with it," he said stiffly. "Actually, it's the only property I own that isn't entailed."

"But to sell the spot where your family first became prominent . . . It seems almost a sacrilege, Aiglon!"

"A sacrilege on top of a desecration," he said, looking all around at the ruins. "It must have been beautiful once. It's built like a proper church—see, this was the nave, and this the transept," he explained, pointing out where cross-ing demarcation lines could still be seen. He walked off to the left. "And this must have been a sort of sacristy. You can see that the walls formed a semicircle extending be-yond the main body of the building. I wonder what it would cost to have it rebuilt."

"That would be a poor investment."

"What price do you put on history?" he asked.

"I was thinking of the imminent sale. You wouldn't get your money back, and, besides, there wouldn't be time to do it."

Aiglon rubbed the back of his neck. I felt he was wa-vering in his notion of selling Thornbury. There was a section of wall that had completely blown away, and he let go my hand and walked out beyond the chapel, where he stood gazing back at it. There was a bemused air about him. I took a last look around the ruined sacristy. I noticed strange little indentations in the soft, grassy earth. Straight bars about two inches long and four inches apart. What could they be? They weren't marks left by any animal or natural force. The marks were too regular, too sharp and clear. I walked forward and examined them. They seemed to go right under a small pile of rocks. I removed a few rocks and saw that the earth there had been recently disturbed.

"Look at this, Aiglon!" I called, and he returned.

"Someone's been trespassing," he commented idly. After all, there wasn't much harm that could be done to a pile of rocks. "Probably poachers. I've seen quite a few rabbits around."

"But what could have made those marks?"

"Possibly the butt of a rifle. I expect they hid their catch under the rocks when they heard someone coming. Are there any old books in the library with sketches of the chapel?" he asked.

"Yes, a few. If you're interested in such things, Aiglon, Rachel bought an old history of the area just the other day. She bought if for you, but it was moldy when she got it home, so she didn't give it to you." I was happy to encourage his interest in the place as it seemed to discourage him selling it. I knew Rachel would be delighted.

"We should mark this day on the calendar. It will be the first time Rachel Savage has ever willingly given anybody anything!" he exclaimed.

"Oh, she's not that bad," I lied.

"If she's been kind to *you*, then I forgive her all the rest. Come, let's go for a drive. It's such a beautiful day."

He took my hand again, and we left the chapel to stroll back through the overgrown path to Thornbury. His groom brought the yellow curricle around, and I was assisted up into it. It's great height and precarious seating seemed less odd and dangerous on this second trip. It was an excellent vehicle for both speed and sightseeing. We drove southwest along the coast road past Folkestone and Hythe. I suggested that we stop at Saltwood Castle, but Aiglon was more eager to continue our drive. With the unappetizing marsh spreading out before us there wasn't much to see, so we turned around and started home.

The traffic was not heavy during the late afternoon, and Aiglon took it into his head that I should have a lesson in what he called "handling the ribbons," which meant driving his team. The team darted along, paying no heed to my restraining orders, but at least they had the wits to remain on the ironed road, so I didn't complain. I sat in silent anguish, frightened to death, while Aiglon merrily told me this was the very thing I needed, a new pastime to alternate with sitting on the pile of rocks and looking at the derelict garden. The excitement put some color into my cheeks, he said. It also blew my hair all over my face and left me breathless, but he was kind enough not to mention those details.

We shot home at a reckless pace till we were just past Folkestone. That is where we met the tranter's wagon, which was removing a house of furniture on a flatbed, drawn by four husky nags. They were an ill-natured team. I'm quite sure Aiglon's grays could have gotten past them without incident if the leader—the tranter's leader, I mean—hadn't decided at that precise moment to stand up on its hind legs and neigh.

The grays had city manners and weren't accustomed to such incivility. They bolted faster, breaking their gait and causing the curricle to jerk dangerously. The reins pulled painfully at my fingers till I was quite sure I had broken one or two of them. I let out a howl of pain sharper than the tranter's neighing nags and dropped the ribbons. This gave the grays the notion that they were to step up their pace even faster. It was very fortunate that Aiglon had the wits to lunge for the dropped reins before they became entangled in the grays' legs or we might have ended up in the nearest field. As it was, we got no farther than the ditch. Nothing was irreparably damaged, not even my pride.

"Why did you pull them off to the right?" I attacked before he could beat me to an accusation.

"It's a little hard to pull straight when you're not in the driver's seat!" he pointed out. "Why did you drop the ribbons? The first lesson you have to learn, Constance, is never to drop the ribbons when your nags are in full gallop."

"No, the first lesson is never to take hold of the ribbons when you don't know how to drive!"

"How are you ever going to become a first-class fiddler if you don't take the ribbons?" he countered.

"I'm not likely to become a first-class fiddler in the space of the day or two you'll be at Thornbury," I reminded him.

"Day or two? I plan to remain till Thornbury is sold. I'll be here for a month at least, possibly through the summer," he said. "Now, take the reins again and get us out of this ditch," he ordered calmly.

"I wouldn't touch them if my life depended on it," I answered, and folded my arms over my chest.

"Driving is like riding. You have to get back in the driver's seat immediately after a little mishap or you'll never regain your nerve. Here, take 'em." He tossed the reins at me and they landed in my lap, where I left them.

Meanwhile, the team was becoming a little restive. They were finding their own way out of the ditch without much trouble. I thought Aiglon would be gentleman enough to take up the reins, but he did nothing of the sort. He just let the nags climb up by themselves and meander down the road. The mishap and their ascent from the ditch appeared to have tired them somewhat, for their pace slackened to about ten miles an hour. This was still faster than I usually drive the gig, but seemed safe compared to the speed of our former dash. When one of the team began eyeing the grass by the roadside, I took up the reins and pulled it into line. We got home without further mishap, but I was as angry as a hornet and determined that I wouldn't subject myself to another ride in Aiglon's fearsome curricle.

"We'll drive east toward Dover tomorrow," he informed me when we reached the stable.

"I've had enough driving for the present," I declared, and hopped down from the perch.

"Would you prefer to ride?" he asked, not displeased with this notion. I saw him looking at his mounts, a pair of vicious-looking brutes pawing the earth in their boxes.

"No, Aiglon, I would prefer to walk. Or, better yet, to stay safely at home!"

He flung the reins to his groom, then took my arm to walk to the house. "That's the wrong attitude. You should always take full advantage of any interesting possibility that comes you way, Constance," he said earnestly. "Now confess the truth: Wasn't the riding lesson more fun than sitting on your rocks?"

"It may seem so someday in retrospect. At the moment, I am tired and hot. My fingers are broken, and my hair is falling into my eyes," I told him.

He stopped and brushed my hair back. "But it's done wonders for your complexion, Constance, my flower. We'll have a glass of wine and a rest, which will take care of the fatigue and the heat."

There was a playful, flirtatious air about him as he made these comments. His head inclined toward mine, his eyes dancing. I was not totally immune to his persuasions, but I was not about to be lured back into the death curricle, either.

"That just leaves my broken fingers," I replied, and tried to resume walking. Aiglon held me immobile with one hand.

"We'll have to get you a thicker pair of gloves. You can wear mine till then. Our hands aren't that different in size," he pointed out, and used this as an excuse to fondle my fingers, stretching them out along his. "Tell me truthfully now, are they really hurt?" he asked.

"Yes, but not broken apparently. Despite the way you're twisting them, I don't hear them cracking."

Then he released my hand and we resumed our walk. "You haven't been heeding my lessons, Constance. The curricle isn't the only object that's been thrown in your path, to be taken advantage of. It also comes with an excellent driver."

He peeped a saucy smile at me. I didn't answer him, for I couldn't think of anything to say. He continued undismayed. "I might as well warn you that I plan to take full advantage of all the beauties of Thornbury, your sweet self included."

We were at the back door. He opened it in silence. I went to my room to survey the travesty of the careful toilette I had begun the excursion in. I looked quite like a dame who had just run a smock race. And won. There was a bright sparkle in my eyes, and my color was certainly enhanced by the outing. There was also a sly smile lifting my lips. Aiglon had managed to ingratiate himself into my good graces.

Despite his drinking and the duel, despite his gambling and the possible sale of the estate—or perhaps because of them—Aiglon was the most interesting man ever to set foot inside of Thornbury, and I would be a fool not to enjoy his presence to the fullest. I hastily cleaned myself up and ran belowstairs to drink the wine prescribed by my new flirt.

CHAPTER SIX

AIGLON HADN'T RETURNED BELOWSTAIRS BY THE TIME I reached the saloon, but Rachel was there. I asked whether she had enjoyed her outing.

"It was completely successful, Constance," she replied, eyes twinkling. "Two Runners inquired after Aiglon. I thought three might be overdoing it. What do you think?"

"I doubt they'd send more than one."

"For a *murder*?" she asked, glaring at me in displeasure. "And what did Aiglon do while I was gone?"

"He took me for a ride in his curricle. We ended in a ditch," I said.

"That sounds exactly like Aiglon. But it *was* wise of you to get him out of the house. He didn't mention noticing anything amiss in my housekeeping?" she inquired warily.

"Nothing of importance," I assured her. "Rachel, with careful handling, I think he might be talked out of selling Thornbury."

"Where do you get that idea?" she asked, keenly interested.

"We were down at the ruined chapel before our drive, and he—"

"What! What the devil were you doing there?" she demanded, her face white with anger or chagrin. I was quite astonished at such a strong reaction.

"Nothing! We were just talking. Why do you look so—so startled?" I asked in confusion.

"That is exactly the isolated sort of place you must keep away from when you're with him, Constance. I feel responsible for you; you were sent here in my charge. A man of Aiglon's kidney—"

"No, really he's not that bad," I objected.

"You must rely on my judgment in this matter. I have known him longer and more intimately than you, my dear. And what gave you the notion he might be dissuaded from selling Thornbury?"

"He is somewhat interested in its historical associations. He mentioned rebuilding the chapel. And naturally he's reluctant to sell the place where his family first rose to prominence. With a little judicious handling, I think he could be talked out of selling." I expected to see joy and to hear congratulations for my news. What I saw was a sharp frown, and what I heard was silence.

At last Rachel spoke. "If he's so badly dipped that he has to sell something, he can't be high enough in the stirrups to rebuild that shambles. I wonder what he's *really* up to."

"It's only a temporary shortage of funds. I have the feeling he acted precipitately in going to Roundtree and that he regrets it already. Give him the book you bought in Folkestone, Rachel, and let us see if we can't kindle his interest in restoring, instead of selling," I urged.

She gave an annoyed *tsk*. "I told you that book was all damp and spotted. In any case, it says very little about Thornbury."

"Well, perhaps there is *something* in the library to do the trick," I offered hopefully. I wondered what was keeping Aiglon so long abovestairs. When Willard shuffled in

67

a little later to speak to Rachel, he told us his lordship had some letters to write.

"He's probably writing to inquire whether he did actually kill that Kirkwell person he shot in the duel or only maimed him for life," Rachel commented.

I was coming to resent Rachel's attitude toward her cousin. It was more likely he was writing to London urging the forwarding of arms for the militia, as he had more or less agreed to do. But that's the way it was with Rachel. When she took someone in dislike, she saw no good in him.

"If he means to poke and pry through the library tonight, I had best make sure it's clean," she said, and went off in that direction, leaving me alone.

It was nearly time for dinner when Aiglon finally came belowstairs and Rachel had returned to the saloon.

"Ah, Aiglon, there you are!" she exclaimed brightly. "Did Constance tell you the dreadful news? I'm afraid you've been found out, my lad. The Runners were in Folkestone this afternoon. Naturally I tried to spread the word I hadn't seen hide or hair of you, but after your visit to Captain Cokewell this morning, it was no use. Rather unwise of you to have sallied forth, was it not?"

Aiglon subjected his cousin to a long, thoughtful gaze that held much derision. "You must be mistaken," he answered mildly. "I had a note from a friend left at General Delivery in Folkestone this morning informing me that Kirkwell is alive and well. They must be after some other villain. Or villainess," he added in a meaningful way, still regarding her steadily.

Rachel's reaction was not at all what I expected. She didn't bridle up in righteous indignation, or laugh, or do anything but return his steady gaze. Some undercurrent flowed between them, some message relayed by Aiglon and assessed by his cousin. My liveliest conjecture brought forth nothing but the larcenous nature of Rachel's house-keeping, and I didn't think this could possibly be a matter for the Bow Street Runners.

"That is good news that you didn't kill Kirkwell, Aiglon," I said, very much relieved to hear it.

I heard Willard's shuffle approaching, heralding the announcement of dinner. Already fumes of poached cod filled the house, killing my appetite. The entire fish, including the head and dress of scales, had been poached and placed on the table. The eye had turned milky and stared at us accusingly as we took our seats.

"Give Lord Aiglon the head," Rachel said to the footman.

It was done, and accepted without a murmur, though I noticed Aiglon immediately reached for the sauceboat and covered the whole thing in the cream sauce that unfortunately accompanied any fish at Thornbury. He picked reluctantly around its edges, occasionally lifting to his lips a forkful of sauce, eked out with mashed potatoes. The sauce was of a consistency that didn't object to a fork. About nine-tenths of the fish was soon removed from the table and replaced by mutton, which was slightly more appetizing.

"I expect you'll be going into town this evening?" Rachel asked Aiglon as we ate.

"No, Constance and I plan to do a little research in the library," he answered.

"That's odd. Miss Pethel has never showed the least interest in the library in the five years she's been here," Rachel answered, mainly for the purpose of showing him he should be calling me Miss Pethel.

"I hope to diversify her interests in more than one direction. How are the fingers, Connie?" he asked, inventing a completely new name for me. I felt ill at ease, having become a pawn between the feuding cousins.

"Not broken after all," I assured him, while Rachel lifted her brows and gave me her displeased look.

"I hear you have a book for me, Cousin" was Aiglon's next line of talk.

"No, no, it's a musty old thing, and of no particular interest," Rachel replied.

"Since it pried loose a few shillings from your reticule, I am most curious to see it," he responded bluntly.

But Rachel turned the conversation to Aiglon's mother and to other relatives who were known to me only by name. When dessert was served, Rachel accepted a plate of bread pudding, but Aiglon, despite having only nibbled at his dinner, was too full to indulge, and so was I. We ladies soon left him to his port and retired to the saloon.

"Since despite my request you saw fit to tell Aiglon about that book I bought, I'd best go and get it," Rachel said. She walked out the door, leaving me alone to ponder the unsettling currents that had formed since Aiglon's arrival. Most of all I disliked being in Rachel's black book. We had been friends for five years, and Aiglon would only be here a short while. I felt I owed her my allegiance, and determined that when she came down with the book I would try to mend the rent in our friendship. I waited for ten minutes, wondering what was taking her so long. For that matter, why had she gone to fetch the book herself instead of sending Willard? She just wanted to get away from me, that's all. And she *hadn't* told me not to tell Aiglon about the book. After waiting a few minutes more, I decided to wait for her in the library. I could begin looking for documents pertinent to the restoration of the chapel.

As I entered the library I was surprised to see that the lamps were already lit, for at Thornbury a lamp isn't generally lit till it is used. I was even more surprised to see Rachel crouching near a bottom shelf, half hidden behind the table. She must have come down by the back stairs to avoid being seen by me.

"Oh, there you are!" I exclaimed. "Rachel, I don't know why you've taken it into your head to think I'm on Aiglon's side. The way you spoke at dinner made me feel quite uncomfortable."

"The way I spoke at dinner, Constance, was for your own good. Before Aiglon came I tipped you the clue that he is a womanizer. I am more determined than ever that he must leave, and the sooner the better."

"But you can't make him go *now*. He didn't kill Kirkwell, so there's no way to make him leave his own house."

She slammed a book on the table. "There's more than one way to skin a cat. Here's the demmed book that you're so determined he should have. I want it made perfectly clear, Constance, that the library door is to be left open the entire time you are in here. Willard will be slouching about in the hall. If you need help, call him."

"Why should I need help?"

"Why do you think?" she asked, piercing me with one of her sharp stares. "Don't make the immature mistake of thinking he means to marry you. I can assure you it is the last thing in his mind."

"And I can assure you it is the last thing in mine!" I replied, equally sharply.

She whisked out the door, and I turned to pick up the book. That's when I noticed it wasn't the book she had bought in Folkestone at all. It was of the same size and color, but I remembered perfectly well the title of that other book. *An Anecdotal History of Folkestone and Environs*, it was called. This one was entitled *Ancient Tales of the Southeastern Counties*. When I opened the cover, I saw it had been marked with the Thornbury stamp, which marked most of the books in the library. I had interrupted her at her work and she hadn't had time to notice the stamp.

I reviewed in my mind the details surrounding the purchase and subsequent history of the Folkestone book, and moment by moment became more intrigued. Mickey Dougherty had brought the book to her attention. He had behaved very peculiarly, too, when he saw her coming out of the used-book store. She had told him she had bought a Bible, and he had said something ambiguous about the "riches" to be found in the Good Book. Was there some clue to "riches" in the Folkestone book? Was this why Rachel so carefully guarded it from Aiglon?

Soon an even worse notion occurred to me. Was this why she didn't want Aiglon to sell Thornbury—and why she was trying to drive down the price so she could buy it herself? This seemed too farfetched to be real, and most unreal of all was that Mickey Dougherty should have let Rachel know of the existence of the book. Why hadn't he bought it himself and found whatever riches were to be found?

As I stood holding the book Rachel had thumped onto the table, other recent and mysterious details occurred to me. Details like Rachel's gathering stones in the rain in my waterproof coat and pattens. She must have been scrabbling about in the mud to have gotten the coat hem soiled. It wasn't so long a coat that the hem dragged, especially with the pattens raising the wearer an inch from the ground with their metal bars. In my mind's eye, I saw those little metal bars, about two inches long and four inches apart, one placed at the toe and one at the heel of each patten. That was the pattern I had seen imbedded in the earth at the ruined chapel! *That's* where Rachel had gone that night—the very night of the day she had bought the Folkestone book and whisked it into her drawer when I went to her room. I was on thorns to see that book and to discover what secret it held. Was it still in her dresser drawer? Certainly it must be somewhere in her room.

I remembered, too, that Mickey Dougherty had paid us a surprising call that evening just after Aiglon's arrival. Rachel had been dismayed to see him. They had held a brief "business" conference in the study, after which they had both emerged, smiling. Some agreement had been struck between them then. Mickey was to get a part of the spoils, probably for his help in doing whatever had to be done to recover the treasure. The next question to think about was what the nature of the treasure or riches could possibly be. But before I had time to consider this problem, Aiglon appeared in the doorway.

He carried a decanter of wine and two glasses, and behind him his own footman bore a platter of fruit, cheese, biscuits, and bonbons.

"Dinner is served, ma'am," said the footman with a bow, and walked in to deposit the treats on the table. Though we had just left the dining room, they were entirely welcome.

"Shiftwell was kind enough to pick up these things for me in town today," Aiglon explained. "My hopes for the kitchen were not high after his report on dinner last night, and I took the precaution of getting in emergency supplies. I shall try to banish the memory of that cod's rebukeful gaze."

Shiftwell nodded in acknowledgment of his part in the affair and departed, leaving the door open behind him.

Aiglon poured two glasses of wine and handed me one. "There is a disreputable French writer called the Marquis de Sade, whom I trust is unknown to you. I fear Rachel has been dipping into his works. She remembers my aversion to cod heads. I had some violent nightmares due to that particular portion of that particular fish when I was a child. Imagine her remembering it after all these years and serving it to me. She really is the limit. To us," he said, lifting his glass and touching it to mine.

We drank a little, then began looking through the shelves for books that might tell us about the chapel. Rachel had told Aiglon that I never went near the library, but in fact it was one of my favorite places at Thornbury. Reading was one pastime that didn't require company, so we both did a fair bit of it. I knew the documents on the building and history of the place were on the lower shelves opposite the doorway and went there to begin the search.

The documents were fading quarto manuscripts, hand-written and illustrated. They included architectural drawings and written history. The handwriting was spidery, and I had never read much of it, but I had seen the drawings any number of times. The chapel had its own folder. I rooted through the little pile, looking for it. I couldn't believe my eyes but it wasn't there. Of course it had been eight months or a year since I had last seen it, but this portion of the shelves was seldom disturbed. I knew in a flash that Rachel had taken it. It hadn't been in her hands when I interrupted her work this evening, but some time in the past two days, since buying that book, she had come here and taken the folder about the chapel from its rightful place. I wasn't prepared to reveal her scheme to Aiglon until I had spoken to her, but I knew it was fruitless to search further.

Aiglon was leafing through the documents with some interest, reading a snatch aloud from time to time between biscuits and cheese and wine, for he was making quite a meal while we worked.

"I can't seem to find the folder on the chapel," I said, arising from my kneeling position.

"That's odd. Everything else is so minutely covered. It must be here somewhere. Let me have a look." He placed me at the lower shelves, and it was my turn to enjoy the treats. The bonbons were delicious, though they made the wine taste sour. After fifteen minutes, Aiglon decided he was not going to find what I had told him wasn't there to begin with and contented himself with looking through other books.

But the history of the time of Edward the Confessor, dealing with the ancient Cinque Ports, was of little interest to either of us. We admired the architect's sketch of Thornbury, and Aiglon pointed out rather more often than was necessary how much better it looked with its gardens in shape. He asserted he could read any hand ever written, but in the end the spider scrawl of his ancestors defeated him, so little actual reading was done.

We had been in the library for over an hour, and propriety decreed that we should return to the saloon to bear Rachel company. I was as reluctant as Aiglon to leave.

"We'll just finish off this last glass of wine before we go," he suggested. I tried to remember whether I'd had two or three glasses. The reason I was interested, of course, was to monitor Aiglon's intake. But really he wasn't in the least bosky. He drank slowly and displayed no signs of overindulgence.

I let him pour the better part of the remains into my glass all the same. "Will you rebuild the chapel if you can find the plans?" I asked.

"Possibly."

"And does that mean that possibly you *won't* be selling Thornbury?" I asked hopefully.

"I wouldn't rebuild if I only meant to sell," he agreed.

I gave him a smile of relief and encouraged this plan, mentioning the importance of maintaining some traces of England's history, the good the building would do to the workers of the area, and other such platitudes as occurred to me.

"Don't mistake me for a philanthropist, Constance," he warned, his eyes flashing mischievously. "I'm only considering it to have something for us to do together. I find sitting on a rock pile less than amusing, and you apparently don't enjoy wrestling with my grays. You may find, when the *Mermaid* arrives, that you're a sailor manqué, and the rebuilding won't be necessary after all."

At this, he drained his glass, and we went forth to the saloon. Rachel wasn't alone, after all. Mickey Dougherty had arrived during our absence and he and Rachel now sat on the sofa, their heads together in deep scheming. Their intriguing attitude confirmed my worst suspicions. Mickey pulled himself to the other side of the sofa when we entered and rose to shake Aiglon's hand.

"Congratulations, Lord Aiglon. I hear your man survived, and you're a decent citizen once again. I was very worried about you," he said.

"Kind of you," Aiglon answered blandly.

"Truth to tell, it wasn't just congratulations on your deliverance that brought me. It was the guns for my militia troop I was worried about. You did post off a letter to London, I trust?"

"I certainly did."

"And you'll be letting us know as soon as you get word they're on their way?"

"Of course," Aiglon replied.

"It was *you* Mickey came to see," Rachel explained to Aiglon before anybody asked her. This might account for Mickey's visit, but it didn't account for the conspiratorial conversation we had interrupted.

After a very brief visit, Mickey rose to leave, and Rachel announced that she was feeling megrimish and would also retire. I rose to follow her upstairs, hoping to discover the whole truth about Mickey's visit.

"If I'm being abandoned, I'll return to the library and have a go at that spiderish writing," Aiglon decided. "I'll have a look at the book you gave me as well, Rachel.

Perhaps you could save me some time and direct me to the chapter dealing with Thornbury?''

"I'm sure I saw a mention of it somewhere," she answered vaguely.

"Probably in the section dealing with Folkestone and Dover," Aiglon said. He made a bow to us and left.

I followed Rachel to her room. "About that book, Rachel, it isn't the one you bought and Aiglon will soon realize it," I warned. "It's stamped with the Thornbury library mark." I regarded her closely to read by her expression what she was thinking, for I well enough knew that she wouldn't say anything revealing till pushed to the wall.

"You're directing your suspicions toward the wrong person, Constance," she answered, her eyes flashing in triumph. "Have a look at this," she said, going to her dresser and pulling a letter from the top drawer. "Perhaps this will convince you what sort of man it is you've been playing up to."

I took the piece of paper and looked at it. I felt a trembling inside even before I'd read a word. It was Rachel's glittering face that frightened me. She looked gloating and victorious, and for her, victory meant getting Aiglon to leave Thornbury.

The letter was brief and catastrophic. It was from the office of the chief of Admiralty Intelligence and said:

My dear Aiglon: This is to notify you that your position with the Government is terminated as of this date. As discussed, we feel it would be better if you retire quietly from London till this unfortunate incident is cleared up. I do not hold you responsible for the capture by the French of the arms intended for the southeast coast, but it is irrefutable that you arranged the shipment and their safe delivery was in your hands.

The rumors will die down if you absent yourself till this

war is over. Our of sight, out of mind. I can't recommend too strongly that you make every effort to conquer that impulse to drink that has caused all your problems. It grieves your dear mother, and I don't have to tell you the harm it does to your own pocket.

Pray forgive my writing you in this frank way. I do it for your own good. I shall miss you in the office.

Kindest regards,

[and the signature]

The letter trembled in my fingers. I had always felt, in the deepest recess of my heart, that Aiglon was much too good for me in the worldly sense. I had half suspected that his flirtation was just that and no more. But I had not been exposed to such city flirtation before and had fallen victim to it. Like any fool falling in love, I had been quick to glance over his shortcomings, to paint over his faults, and to seek a glimmer of virtue. Now the truth was before me in black and white. My real anger was for Aiglon, but it was only Rachel who was there to receive it and I turned an icy face to her.

"Where did you get this, Rachel?" I asked, as though she were my underling and had better have a good excuse to explain herself.

"In the bottom of Aiglon's drawer, hidden under his linen. He had concealed it well, you may be sure."

"I daresay he didn't expect to have his private belongings searched in his own house!" I sniffed.

"I know where my duty lies, if you don't!" she informed me, then reached out and pulled the letter from my fingers. "I've given a quick search to his jacket pockets and other things as well. I was hoping for some clue as to with whom he might be working."

"You mean you rifled all his private belongings! Really, Rachel, you have no shame," I scoffed, but some base part of me was eager to learn what else she might have discovered.

"Certainly I did, and I'm not ashamed of it. You see why he told us that Banbury tale of having killed a man. It was to cover this! He either sold information about that arms shipment to the French or he was so drunk they got it out of him. Either way, he is a scoundrel and no fit company for us. And to think he sat there with his sly smile, telling Mickey he had sent word to Whitehall to ship more arms. As though they would let him know if they did! They've sent him packing. He came running to this out-of-the-way place to hide his head in shame."

"He must have been drunk. He would never be so low as to sell arms or information to the French," I insisted, but it was only bravado speaking.

"Bah, his own grandmother is as French as brandy. He brags of it. You heard him yourself, speaking to Mickey. Certainly he sold that information to the French, and his superior knows it full well. He is only being polite in deference to Lady Aiglon. You don't terminate a *lord's* employment for no more serious a reason than taking a little too much wine. Lord, they all do that! No, Constance, what we harbor under our roof is a *traitor*."

My throat felt dry. "What are you going to do?" I asked.

"I plan to return this letter to its proper spot and say nothing, but I shall keep a sharp eye on Aiglon. You see now why he is making up to Mickey Dougherty. He wants to learn when the next shipment is coming so that he may sell that information to the Frenchies as well. We'll be shot in our beds with English weapons. Was there ever such a villain in the world!"

"That letter doesn't say anything of the sort!" I reminded her, and tried to console myself.

"I'll tell you something, miss! Aiglon was not playing

cards at the inn last night as he told me he was. He was in Madame Bieler's saloon, and we all know what *she* is!''

"A widow, you mean, or that she sells Mickey's stuff?" I asked. A widow, in Madame's case, implied a good deal more than that she had survived a husband. I'm not sure whether she ever actually had a husband, but a married woman had more latitude in the matter of entertaining gentlemen without the inconvenience of a chaperone. Madame entertained a great many gentlemen, at all hours of the night.

"Ninnyhammer! I mean that she is *French*! She is probably putting Aiglon in touch with other Frenchies who will buy any other secrets he has for sale. I begin to think it is we who must leave Thornbury, Constance. My nerves can't take much more of this."

I looked again at the fateful letter she still held. "You'd better put his letter back," I said, and walked out the door.

When I had gone up those stairs, I'd had every intention of returning below to the library again, but I put any such idea out of my mind now. I even forgot to ask Rachel about that stupid book. It was only a trifle compared to the awful knowledge I now unwillingly carried. It felt as heavy as a ton of coal on my heart. Beautiful, shining, smiling Aiglon was either such a confirmed drunkard that he had witlessly betrayed his country, or he was a willing traitor. Not half an hour before, I had convinced myself that he didn't have a serious drinking problem. So he had sold or given his knowledge of the arms shipment to the French with full knowledge, and he had come scrambling down to Folkestone to get new information indirectly since it was no longer available to him legally.

Of course he wouldn't leave Thornbury willingly when it was such an excellent base for discovering dangerous secrets. He didn't care a groat about the ruined chapel. He just wanted an excuse to hang about. The only question in my mind was why he had spoken to Roundtree about selling the house. He must really be short of funds as well. He could put up at an inn and live on the proceeds from the sale until his next quarter allowance came along to be squandered as well.

And this was the gentleman whose attentions, if the whole truth were to be said, I had been flattered to death to be receiving. I wanted to rush downstairs and chastise him while my fury was at its peak, but I didn't feel up to this. I just sat on the edge of my bed looking at the dresser without seeing it. I felt ten years older than when I had gotten up that morning.

CHAPTER SEVEN

I DIDN'T RETURN BELOWSTAIRS AT ALL THAT EVENING, and I didn't hear Rachel go down, either. Her room, however, was at the far end of the corridor, and she sometimes went down by the servants' stairs without my hearing her. What I really was listening for was Aiglon's ascent. At midnight, I was still listening. And at one o'clock in the morning. It was some time after two when his stumbling steps along the corridor roused me from a fitful sleep. He was singing rather loudly. I heard his faithful valet open his bedroom door and try to shush him. This disgusting display hardened further my heart against Aiglon, but as I lay in the darkness listening, the insidious thought arose that perhaps drunkenness was his only sin. Drink might have led him into that duel and be accountable for his being a traitor as well. It was bad, but not as bad as willfully selling out his country.

At breakfast the next morning, Rachel bluntly informed me that I looked like "something the cat had dragged in." Such was my mood that I replied with equal frankness that she looked like death warmed-over herself. She did, too. There were hollows below her eyes and lines running from her nose to her lips. After this exchange of compliments, we turned to the cause of our state—Aiglon's behavior.

"He came staggering in at two-thirty this morning, completely disguised," I told her. "What are we going to do about him, Rachel? We'll have to report him to the authorities. We can't let him roam the countryside learning secrets to sell to the French. Though I doubt if he could learn much, the way he drinks."

"Report him and bring disgrace on the family? Impossible!" she decreed. "Mind you, his drinking doesn't interfere with the full use of his wits. All the Howells can operate efficiently when they are foxed. His papa used to speak for hours in the House, then retire to his chamber and fall down flat from drink. No, we can't report him, Constance. We must catch him and put a stop to it ourselves."

"And how do you propose we do that, just the two of us? Or do you think we should ask some close, reliable male friend to help us? Lord Ware, perhaps? But he's in London half the time. I'm sure Mickey would enjoy it," I added doubtfully.

A tinkle of laughter floated over the table. "Mickey Dougherty?" she asked. "I'd stake my nose he's in on it with Aiglon by now. I'd no sooner trust him than I'd trust a footpad with my diamonds."

"But he's very active in the militia," I reminded her.

"Of course he is! That's where he recruits his Gentlemen to run brandy. How is it possible you've lived here for five years, Constance, and have no notion what's going on under your very nose?"

"It's not going on under my very nose! I've never even seen the militia practice. How did you discover that's where he recruits his men?"

"He boasts of it, the rogue! No, you and I must handle this business ourselves, Constance."

"That's patently ridiculous. Aiglon's out half the night. And with his fast curricle and faster mounts there's no way we could keep up with him in any case," I pointed out. Really, Rachel could develop the most ludicrous schemes.

"I shouldn't worry too much about the late-night rambles. He is visiting Madame Bieler, and it has nothing to do with discovering state secrets," she announced blandly. "Their liaison has been arranged to mutual satisfaction, I understand. Mickey let something slip last night."

It was easy to believe her. It was coming to the point where I would believe any evil of Lord Aiglon. My reply was sulky. "I still don't see how you think we can stop him."

"You underestimate me, Constance," she replied with hateful hauteur. "Steps have already been taken. I have spoken to his servants, who are worried about him and eager to help. Indeed, Shiftwell told me he had been about to enlist my aid. Groom, valet, footmen—they are all our allies. As Aiglon seems quite determined to add you to his list of flirts, you might as well indulge him. So long as he has his Madame Bieler to expend his stronger instincts, your virtue will be safe, and you can keep your eyes and ears open to discover what you can. You never know—he might be indiscreet enough to let something slip. I, of course, shall keep a sharp eye on any letters he receives or sends."

"I don't want to have anything to do with him," I said firmly.

"Consider it your little mite to help the war cause, Constance. This is not a time for selfishness. I do wish you'd keep him away from the chapel, however. Let him teach you to ride and drive," she suggested.

"Speaking of the chapel, Rachel," I began as I remembered my thoughts in that regard, "are you afraid Aiglon will find the treasure?"

"Treasure? What treasure is that, dear?" she asked, cool as a cucumber.

"The treasure mentioned in that book you bought, which

you refuse to give to Aiglon," I replied with a knowing stare.

"Oh, that! Yes, my hopes were raised for a day or two, but nothing came of it. The book said there were gold chalices and monstrances and things in the chapel. It was a Roman Catholic chapel at the time, you know. I went down and moved the rocks about a little but found nothing. You can have the book now if you want it. Shall I get it for you?" This offer convinced me she was telling the truth, and I declined.

Her next suggestion was that I go abovestairs and try on her old riding habit since I hadn't one of my own. I was to be ready to accompany Aiglon on any outing he suggested except going to the chapel. As I considered it, this presented a little mystery.

"Why don't you want Aiglon going to the chapel, Rachel?" I asked. "And don't tell me it's the isolation that concerns you. You're willing enough to let me go riding through fields with him and that can be even more isolated."

"Well, to tell the truth, I sold two loads of rock the year before you came. If Aiglon takes it into his head to be rebuilding the chapel, he'll notice the shortage and begin asking bothersome questions. How was I to know he would ever rebuild the place? I thought I was doing him a favor to get rid of the mess," she told me. It sounded so exactly like her that I didn't have to inquire further. It occurred to me that a criminal strain ran deep in the Howell family.

Aiglon slept late after his strenuous night with Madame Bieler. I had ample time to try on Rachel's riding habit, to have it brushed and aired and pressed. It was a deep mulberry shade, made up in serge. The cut of it was not the highest kick of fashion, but Rachel's sense for clothes is so good that it would never be entirely passé. It had a short, fitted jacket and a full, flaring skirt. The collar and front were piped with black ribbon, and the buttons were of jet. A rather dashing black bonnet with ribbons accompanied the outfit. The habit was hung in my closet, where I eyed it impatiently, for it looked better on me than most of my own gowns.

Aiglon came to the table for lunch, unrepentant and unmarked by his late-night revels. "Another lovely day!" he said, looking out the windows to where the sunshine filtered through the leaves of an old mulberry tree, which defied time and went on blooming forever. "I feared an endless spring of clouds and showers here on the coast, but your weather is better than London's."

Rachel had tired of punishing us all with fish, and we enjoyed a meal of cold ham and mutton, Stilton and mustard. We had no pinery, so no pineapples, oranges or other fresh fruits were served, but the plum preserves did as well. The food looked appetizing, but when I tried to eat, it tasted like wood. I looked at Aiglon and couldn't believe that such a villain's mind was wrapped in that hero's head.

"Are you prepared for another lesson with the grays today, Constance?" he asked cordially.

"If you like," I answered, stiff as starch. Rachel nudged my ankle under the table, and I added, "That sounds lovely. Where shall we go?"

"Let us go to Madame Bieler's and order you a riding habit," he suggested without so much as a blush at mentioning that woman's name at a polite table.

"That won't be necessary, Aiglon," Rachel bounced in before I uttered any of the retorts that rose to my tongue. "We have discovered that mine fits her perfectly."

"Excellent! Then we shall ride instead," he decided.

I looked at my ham, pale and sliced as thin as paper, and pushed it aside.

"Do you have some objection, Constance?" Aiglon asked, gazing at me, concern or a question in his eyes.

"No, but you'll have to be patient. I haven't ridden since the last time I was home—months ago."

"Once a rider, always a rider," Rachel assured me. "Where will you go?"

"I'd like to ride along the beach," Aiglon said, and looked at me for agreement.

There seemed little possibility for mischief in this, so I agreed.

Immediately after lunch I changed into the riding habit. The lady in the mirror looked fashionable, calm, and sure of herself, but inside I was a welter of unresolved emotions. I didn't much want to be in Aiglon's private company. I didn't trust that innocent heart of mine, which wasn't accustomed to the cajoling of an experienced flirt. I didn't even want to help Rachel trap him, but I knew that it was my duty and girded my loins to do it.

Rachel was waiting in the hallway when I came downstairs. "I'll have a good search of his room while you're gone," she whispered. "Keep him for a couple of hours if you can. He's waiting out front."

The sun and newly leafed trees mocked my heavy heart. It was a day made for romance, possibly even for falling in love. And Aiglon stood with the sun streaking behind him, giving his black head an iridescent halo. He smiled with approval at my new style. I lifted my skirts and went toward him. He had taken my mount to the steps so that I might have a mounting block. The animal was a gray dappled mare, deep-chested, long-legged, but with a kindly eye. I was relieved not to be expected to ride the other horse, an enormous black gelding with eyes like a devil.

"Miranda's a sweet goer. She won't give you any trouble," he promised. He helped me into the saddle and then mounted his own horse.

I experienced no fear or discomfort at being on horse-

I experienced no fear or discomfort at being on horseback again after such a long time. "Has Miranda any tricks I should know about?" I asked.

"She's a follower, not a leader. I'll hold Ariel in check, and she'll be fine." He turned and began trotting down the path to the main road. I fell in beside him.

"They're named from Shakespeare's *The Tempest*, are they?"

"Yes, and they have a relative called Caliban who inherited all the vice in the family."

"Rather like you in the Howell family," I replied.

He took it for a prime joke and laughed, fixing me with a flash from his dark eyes. "I'm glad to see your spirits are restored. I thought you seemed a trifle off at lunch. I was hoping to see you again last night. Do you always retire so early?" His tone was completely normal, friendly, and innocent.

"No, not usually."

"It was the unusual exertion of driving that tired you, perhaps?" he asked. I attempted a smile instead of a verbal reply. "You'll fall fast asleep in the middle of dinner this evening, I expect."

"Very likely. Did you have any success in deciphering the spiderish writing in the library after I left? You *did* say that's what you were going to do, didn't you?"

"Very little luck," he answered. "But, to tell the truth, I didn't stay long at it. I decided to give my card partners the chance to earn back their losses of the night before."

Choked with anger at this easy lie, I said nothing but rode on. "If you'd like to canter, give Ariel his head. You've already told me he sets the pace," I said. Less conversation was necessary at a faster pace.

"Sure you can hack it?" he asked. On my assurance that I could, he let Ariel out, and we soon reached the main road, from which we continued down to the beach.

I had never ridden on the beach before. It was delightful. The cool ocean breeze was refreshing, and the waves came in strongly, washing and gurgling a yard from us. There were no fences or ditches, just a smooth stretch of shore. The unimpeded run allowed us to enjoy the view of the ocean, where a few fishing boats coasted, their sails billowing in the wind. I'm sure Eden was nothing like it, but this beach instilled a feeling of peace and innocence and beauty. And, of course, both places had their viper, too.

"Are you game for a short gallop?" Aiglon called. We had drifted a few yards apart. His voice was scarcely audible above the music of the waves. I nodded and held on more tightly to Miranda's reins. Ariel spurted ahead, and soon Miranda was after him. It was exhilarating: the wind on my face, the tang of salt on my lips when a bit of foam blew upward. Every atom of my body was alive. I felt like Bellerophon riding his Pegasus to heaven. I wished we could go on riding and riding and never have to stop. At one point, Miranda took it into her head to be the leader, and as I pulled past Aiglon, I saw the reckless smile that curved his lips, the tense, alert set of his head and shoulders, and winced to think that only hours before he had been stumbling drunkenly up the stairs. And in another twelve hours, he would, in all probability, be doing the same again.

Aiglon turned his head to me and called, "Race?"

But Miranda's moment of daring was already over. Ariel darted on, and I let the distance between us lengthen. When Aiglon reached an outcropping of rock, he stopped and waited for me. He was breathing hard, and I found to my surprise that I was panting.

"You're doing pretty well for someone who doesn't ride!" he complimented.

"I used to do a fair bit of it."

"Do you hunt?"

"When we go to Westleigh, I'll fix you up with a hunter," he said calmly, as though my going to Westleigh were the most natural thing in the world.

He must have seen the shocked look on my face, for he rushed to explain the remark. "It's not that far away, you know. I thought we all—you, Rachel, and I—might take a run over there one of these days. I have a little business there to tend to. Excellent rocks for garden gazing," he added, and smiled winningly.

It sounded less shocking now that he explained it, and my heartbeat settled down to normal. I had to wonder why he would dash off to Westleigh if he were involved in any treasonous dealings. Surely he would want to stay here, to keep an ear to the ground for news of arms shipments.

"Let's gallop back," he said, and we did, with the same sensations as before.

When we reached the part of the beach close to Thornbury, Aiglon suggested we dismount and walk for a while. I was tired enough, so this sounded agreeable. As there was nowhere to tether the horses, we held the reins and they walked behind us. Soon Aiglon reached out and took my hand in his.

"This is doing me any amount of good," he said simply.

I took it as an oblique remark on his professed reason for coming to Thornbury, which was to remove himself from wicked company and thereby reform. It galled me that he could utter such deceitful words, and in this idyllic setting, too.

I turned a reproachful face to him. "It will all be undone tonight, though, when you go to play cards again. Don't tell me two small ales were all you had last night!" Naturally I wished to say a good deal more, but I couldn't reveal the worst of what we knew concerning his activities with Madame Bieler.

He stopped walking and looked down at me. Contrition and shame warred on his face. "I wouldn't have gone at all if you had come back downstairs," he replied. "Help me, Constance. You could cure me if you thought it worth your while," he urged. The reins fell from his hand, and he took a close grip on my fingers. "Let me make it worth your while," he added, putting his arms around me right there on the public beach. I pushed him away as though he were a demon and took a careful look around to make sure we were completely alone. His gaze followed mine, and the look he gave me spoke of our privacy.

"Make it worth Madame Bieler's while!" I shot back angrily, and scrambled back up on Miranda's back with no help from my escort.

I led Miranda away, and soon Aiglon was beside me on Ariel. He didn't attempt any conversation, but his expression looked very thoughtful. I assumed he was preparing some explanation and was quite willing to hear it. We crossed the road back to Thornbury and proceeded along the road that slices through the park. When we were half-way to the house, Ariel turned off to the left and Miranda followed. It was possible to reach the stables by this route, though it was no shorter than staying on the road. I soon learned Aiglon wasn't heading to the stables but to the ruined chapel. When he got there, he dismounted and tied Ariel to a tree.

My instinct was to continue home, but with Rachel's command to keep him away for a couple of hours ringing in my ears, I decided to stop and hear what he had to say. Aiglon held Miranda's head while I hopped down. His other arm was out to assist me. Before my toes touched the ground, he had swept me into his arms for a heady embrace. It was no mere kiss, but a crushing assault on all my senses. The kind of kiss a woman, alone at night, dreams of. It was the kiss of a bandit or a pirate, demand-

my senses. The kind of kiss a woman, alone at night, dreams of. It was the kiss of a bandit or a pirate, demanding and wild, hot on the lips and setting the blood singing. Primitive urges stirred in me as I felt the hard wall of his chest shaping my body to his, with those muscled arms holding me fast. I heard the leaves above whisper in the breeze, heard the harness jingle as Miranda pawed the ground in disapproval, smelled the sweet scent of wildflowers and the more pungent aroma of the horses to remind me it was real and not a dream. The kissing bandit had the expertise of a Casanova, moving his lips in irresistible ways that set my toes tingling. Yet there was something of a Romeo in him as well. A yearning, hopeless something. Or was that my own small contribution to the kiss?

Then it was over. Aiglon stepped back and looked warily down at me. "You shouldn't have looked so adorably prudish. I couldn't resist" was his apology, or explanation.

He looped Miranda's reins around a tree beside Ariel, and we walked, as though by prearrangement, back to the rocks we had sat on the day before. I sat down, completely mute, and Aiglon sat beside me, his arm loosely around my waist.

He inclined his dark head to mine and looked at me for a longish while. When he spoke, his voice was normal— not angry or apologetic or anything but normal. "Was it you or Rachel who found the letter?" he asked.

"What letter? What are you talking about?" I asked, even as the blood rose up in my neck, and my eyes faltered in their attempt to meet his.

"The letter that is missing from my top drawer."

"I told her to put it back!" I gasped, horrified that Rachel should be so negligent.

"She did, but in her haste she put it in the wrong drawer. I was ready to assume Rachel was the culprit, but it seemed unlike her to make such an obvious mistake. Are you saying it wasn't you?''

"I wouldn't dream of doing such a thing, Aiglon!"

"But you read it? Rachel showed it to you?"

"Yes, but I didn't know at the time where she'd found it.''

"What a sweet innocent you are, Constance," he said, pushing a stray strand of hair back from my forehead. "We're talking about *my* alleged treason, and you worry that I suspect *you* of a bit of snooping. I was hoping Rachel hadn't showed you the letter," he said reluctantly.

"What happened, Aiglon? Was it you who . . ."

"Sold out to the Frenchies?" he asked, his voice hard. "Not likely! I have a brother on the Peninsula. The letter didn't accuse me of *that*!"

"But you were responsible for the safe delivery of the arms," I reminded him.

"I don't know how it happened. I just don't know how word got out about the shipment. The guns were loaded at night aboard a ship with a cargo of pig iron from Bristol. The guns were packed in the same cartons as the iron. The only ones who knew the time of the shipment were the army and the militia here at Folkestone. If word was leaked to the Gentlemen or the French, it had to happen here at this end.''

"Maybe you were drunk and let something slip," I suggested.

"No, I'd remember if I had," he insisted.

"You were drunk for two days when you had the duel with Kirkwell," I reminded him.

"Yes, but I remember every minute of it! I only drank so much at that time because of the lost arms. I felt culpable, but not guilty of willful wrongdoing." His head drooped and a weary sigh escaped his lips.

I felt more sorry for him than condemnatory. "At least

His head bounced up, his eyes opened wide. "Is that what you think!" he exclaimed, stunned. "Good God, I wonder that you even speak to me! Constance, I'm not *that bad*! The reason I am here is to try to discover who did this wretched thing and bring him to justice."

"Wouldn't the Isle of Wight be a more likely place to look?"

"I've been there. The trail leads to Folkestone. If I'm any judge of men, the folks in Wight hadn't a notion what was on that ship. Rumor there is that it was an outside job. The sailors standing guard that night got drunk on brandy. No English ship would have anything aboard but rum, and even that's rationed. Someone smuggled brandy to them. That suggests an involvement by either the Gentlemen or the French. Of course, here on the coast, brandy isn't that hard to come by."

"Even Rachel buys it," I told him.

"Yes, but I assume Rachel didn't know the arms were at Wight. The only ones who knew that were the army and the militia. I don't think either of those bodies are responsible, but someone discovered the secret from them."

"Mickey is both a smuggler and a militiaman," I said, thinking aloud.

"I'm keeping an eye on Mickey. I've noticed he frequently asks when another shipment might be expected. On the other hand, he's sharp enough that I don't think he'd make an issue of it if he were involved. He's more devious than that, don't you think?"

"He has more turns than the coast of England. He'd never deal directly if a more roundabout way were possible," I admitted. "And how will you try to catch the criminals, Aiglon?"

"When the arms are on their way and the route decided, I'll be watching," he said vaguely.

"When the arms are on their way and the route decided, I'll be watching," he said vaguely.

"But you won't know. The officials in London wouldn't tell you because of . . . of what happened the last time."

A stormcloud gathered on his handsome brow. "I still have a few friends at Whitehall who don't think me a traitor," he answered curtly. "Of equal importance to me, Constance, is, what do *you* think?" he asked, and gazed at me, waiting for my answer.

"I don't think you would purposely sell arms to the French. I didn't know you had a brother in Spain. Rachel never mentioned it."

"That's because he has nothing she can steal from him," he replied, and laughed ironically. "I mean to give Thornbury to him when he returns—give him the use of it, I mean."

"Then you never planned to sell it at all!" I exclaimed.

"You don't miss much, do you, my flower? No, of course I could never sell Thornbury. I shall bring it into livable shape before turning it over to Nicholas, though."

"Why did you speak to Roundtree about selling it?"

"I deemed it a clever notion to put about the story that I'm desperate for money. Desperate men will do awful things—like sell out their country. Especially if someone were to take the notion I'd already sold out once and was in need of funds, he might think it worthwhile to approach me with a proposition," he explained. There was a playful expression on his face at odds with the seriousness of the charge against him. No one here knew what was said of him in London; the letter was the only clue.

I sat staring, my mind alive with the most pleasant conjectures. "Do you mean it's all a hoax, that letter from Whitehall? You never were responsible for losing that shipment at all? Is that it, Aiglon?" I asked eagerly, hopefully.

He wouldn't tell me, but the smile that graced his lips

an incriminating document lying about instead of destroying it if there weren't a very good reason?" he asked.

"But who was to see it, hidden beneath your linens?"

"I counted on Willard, or Meg, or Rachel herself. Mind you, I didn't count on meeting someone whom I would hate to have such a bad opinion of me. You mustn't breathe a word of this, Constance."

"Oh, no, I shan't, Aiglon, but neither will Rachel. If you want that story to get abroad, you'll have to think of something else."

"Yes, I must get quite bosky this evening at the White Hart and let the letter fall out of my pocket. I didn't want to rush things, you know. First I establish my insobriety, then I drop the letter. It's more credible that way, and there's no great hurry. The shipment won't be coming for a few days yet."

I stared at his healthy, vibrant young face. "I knew you couldn't be an habitual drunkard. Do you go stumbling out of the White Hart at night, too, the way you stumble up the stairs at home?"

"Certainly I do. I considered sobering up before I got home, but servants are such excellent tattletales that I didn't want my conduct at Thornbury to be startlingly different from what it is abroad," he explained.

"You really should tell Rachel. She's very worried."

"I'd like to, but she sees a good deal of Mick Dougherty. She might refute some other notions I've been carefully planting in his head. He talks to so many people, you know, that he's one of the main sources of gossip in town. I've done such a thorough job of convincing him I'm a reprobate that he's already offered to take me on a run to France on the *Mermaid* when she arrives." He shook his head and laughed at what strange twists this double life was leading him into.

I smiled, too, with relief and joy. Aiglon was what he

always seemed to be to me. An upstanding gentleman, even heroic and gallant. And here he sat with me, Constance Pethel, on a rock in the garden at Thornbury, soon speaking again of our visit to Westleigh. Anything could happen in the next week or two. It was even possible that when Aiglon left for good, I might go with him.

It was one of the happiest afternoons of my life. A sort of calm before the storm, but I didn't know that then. I only knew I was fast falling in love, and I thought Aiglon was, too.

CHAPTER EIGHT

LOVE IS BLIND, AND THOUGH I WAS ENAMORED, I WAS still able to see that Aiglon was an extremely accomplished liar. How glibly he had explained the interwoven series of lies to me before he broke down and confessed the delightful truth. The condemning letter from the Admiralty was a hoax—there was no treachery, no drunkenness, and no gambling. The lie about planning to sell Thornbury was to buttress the lie that he was short of money. He was a man who could lie his way out of hell, and it disturbed me that he had such a facility for lying. Perhaps his fondness for me was a lie as well? What reason would he have for this implied lie? He hadn't actually said in words that he cared for me. Was I being buttered up in preparation for some part in his scheme? Surely not! My every instinct rejected the very idea, but some measure of cold reason remained.

I listened carefully to every word Aiglon said during dinner. He was teasing Rachel about selling Thornbury, asking if she had made up her mind where she would go to live instead. It could have been construed as cruelty, had he not already told me that he would offer her a flat in London. Of course, Rachel was getting off pretty lightly, considering all the stunts she had played on Aiglon over the years.

He joined us in the saloon after dinner for half an hour. First Rachel was urged to take a seat at the clavichord, then I. Rachel could play well and enjoyed playing for company, so I was surprised when she declined, and in no polite way, either. I don't play at all and declined more politely. Rachel was restless that evening. I put it down to ill humor over losing her sinecure at Thornbury.

When the conversation flagged, Aiglon announced his intention of taking a run into Folkestone. I was sorry but resigned. Rachel couldn't conceal her delight. As soon as he went upstairs to prepare himself, she left the saloon, and I waited alone, hoping for a word with Aiglon before he left. It was the matter of Madame Bieler that kept me there. Of course he would say he was going to the inn to see what he could learn about the stolen shipment of arms, but his way with a lie troubled me.

"You're off to the White Hart, are you?" I asked when he came down, dressed for outdoors.

"Duty before pleasure, alas!" he said, sweeping me an elegant bow. "Why couldn't you have been a man, Constance, so you could come with me? Or even a lady of less stringent propriety," he added.

"Like Madame Bieler, you mean?" I asked, happy to have found a quick and plausible way of mentioning her name.

"No, I couldn't wish to see you so changed as all that!" he exclaimed, and laughed lightly.

"You've met her then?" I was becoming somewhat adept at implying a lie myself, for I knew that he had, but tried to sound surprised.

"In the course of business only. I'm having myself a new gown made up" was his facetious explanation.

"She's very pretty." I mentioned this offhandedly but took a sharp look to read his expression.

"She is, and, more important, she is very French," he pointed out. There was a meaningful look in his eyes.

"Is she in on it, Aiglon?" I asked. This was a startling idea despite her nationality. Madame had been here before I arrived at Thornbury five years ago. She was such an excellent seamstress that her being French was overlooked. She didn't seem at all the kind of woman to be involved in anything dangerous. She was so exquisitely feminine. Of course, she retailed the silk and small lots of brandy for Mickey, but there was no danger for her in that.

She was completely an indoors woman. One seldom saw her on the streets. So far as the feminine citizens were concerned, she lived in her shop, and the men would only enlarge her horizons to her saloon. She didn't receive feminine callers in a social way. She was petite, elegant, and cultivated in accent and speech. It would be hard to imagine a less likely criminal, unless it should be myself.

"That is what I'm endeavoring to find out," he replied.

"You've been to her house, then?"

"I dropped in for a few minutes with Mickey one evening. She doesn't trust me yet. She served us tea," he said.

"I see." I disliked the prissy sound of my own voice.

"Now don't be like that, Constance," he wheedled, taking my hand and squeezing it. "It won't be for long, you know. Why don't you plan a picnic for us tomorrow afternoon? We'll have another lesson with the grays."

This was some consolation. "All right. Where would you like to go?"

"Surprise me," he suggested. His eyes glowed, and his lips parted in a smile, revealing a flash of white teeth. "The destination is not important; it's the company I look forward to. *A demain, ma fleur petite.*" On this outburst of French, he lifted my hand to his lips and kissed the knuckles.

"It is the current style in London to offer the open hand

for osculation, Constance, not the fist," he informed me, biting back a laugh. "Like so." He pried my fingers loose and kissed the palm of my hand, holding it a moment against his face. His chin and cheeks were perfectly smooth. At these close quarters, I noticed a pleasant scent of cologne emanating from him. I didn't think these were preparations to seduce the gentlemen at the White Hart.

This done, he cocked his curled beaver at a rakish angle over his eye and left, with a flourish of cane and walking stick. I looked out the window, noticing that he entered his traveling carriage, not the curricle. I was unhappy to think of him going off, possibly to visit Madame Bieler, but I consoled myself with tomorrow's picnic.

I went to the kitchen to speak to Meg about a lunch. We always took roast squab on our picnics at home. I imagined myself with Aiglon under the trees at some picturesque spot, perhaps the grounds of one of the local castles that were open to the public. We would have wine, cheese, bread, and some of Cook's wonderful sweets. The subject of Madame Bieler would not arise. He would tell me about his brother, Nicholas, and I'd tell him about Prissy and my other sisters and brothers. Perhaps a discreet mention that Prissy, my younger sister, was on the verge of marriage . . .

"There's no squabs in the house," Meg said in her surly way. "What you've got is ham and mutton. There's an end of Stilton, not too dry and hard. It's not my day for making bread. What I made yesterday will have to do. Do you want some of the wizened apples put into the basket?"

"No, thank you, Meg. But do you think you could make some cream buns or perhaps your delicious apple tart?"

"I've just made a plum cake. Who's to eat that if I go making up apple tarts?" she demanded. "I've got a dozen mouths to feed, with all his lordship's fine servants ordering up gammon and eggs all hours of the day. I've only got ten fingers, miss. It's eight by the clock, and not a dish is in the water yet from dinner. I'm a servant, not a slave!''

"You're right, Meg. The plum cake will be fine. Where's Willard? I'll want some wine from the cellar.''

"He's up with the mistress. And *he's* ragged as well, poor soul.''

"I'll get the wine," I said to appease her, for I could see that she was up to her elbows in work.

I took a tallow candle, lit it, and opened the door to the cellar. It was as black as midnight down there, but I left the door open behind me. Before I descended one step, Meg banged it shut, complaining of a draft. I descended into the bowels of the cellar, not afraid, for I'd been there dozens of times and knew the wine racks were close to the bottom of the stairs. I wanted a claret for the meat and a Madeira for afterward.

I found the claret with no trouble and proceeded along the racks toward the end, where the sweet wines were kept. My candle flame was unsteady in the damp, drafty cellar. Its acrid odor was in my nose, and I knew the smoke from the tallow was blacker than it was from beeswax, though I couldn't see it. The top racks were empty, and I crouched down, lowering my candle to read the labels. I didn't want a Marsala, only a good Madeira. Something peculiar struck my ear as I crouched in the darkness. It sounded fearfully like the rustle of a rodent just behind the racks. I set down the bottle of claret, held the candle higher, and peered around the end of the racks. There was a suspicious feeling of motion, but in the shadows I couldn't actually see anything. It was only a sound and perhaps a movement of air. The sound was heavier than what a rat or a mouse would make, however. I thought it must be Bijou, Meg's cat, who is occasionally put down to chase the mice.

Meg had been so busy the past few days that it was

possible she had forgotten all about Bijou. The poor thing might be thirsty and lonesome. "Here, kitty. Come, Bijou," I called, taking a step forward. The motion was repeated, retreating now. I looked around the little puddle of lighted area, moving my candle to and fro, wondering why Bijou should be afraid of me. I saw a black leather bag, not unlike a doctor's satchel, on the floor. I had never seen it before and was curious enough to lift it. It was very heavy. From within, a metallic sound could be distinguished, possibly a doctor's instruments. It was an unusual thing to come across in a cellar, particularly since no doctor had ever inhabited Thornbury as far as I knew. I tried the fastener and found that it was not rusted as I thought it would be. It slid open fairly easily. I was just about to open it wide when a pair of black arms flashed out at me. From somewhere above the arms came a ferocious growling sound.

I dropped both satchel and candle and ran for my life. All I could think of was a bogeyman, that imaginary character invented to frighten children. Unreal, that was how it seemed to me. But the single golden coin that fell out of the satchel was not imagined. It plinked with the sound of metal money and rolled in a circle. I ran, screaming, up the stairs into the unwelcoming presence of Meg.

"What's the matter then, rats?" she asked, scowling. "I'll put Bijou down there tomorrow, see if I don't."

"A man!" I managed to squeak out. "There's a man down there, Meg."

"Woosha," she said, unbelieving. "How would a man get past me in the kitchen? There's nobody down there but a shadow."

Still, she called Willard before returning below. Emboldened by their presence, I went with them, telling my story as I went. My guttered candle was on the floor behind the wine racks to substantiate my tale, but of the satchel there was no trace. The possibility of one sole coin still being somewhere on the floor, however, induced Meg to make a thorough search, and there, just under the edge of the wine rack, was the guinea.

"Well, as I live and breathe!" she exclaimed, delighted with her find. "Take a look at this, Willard." She bit it and declared it to be genuine. The most complete search of the cellar did not discover the mother lode from which it had come, but it did reveal that the outside cellar door was unlocked. It locked from the inside, and was always kept locked. A stranger's entrance by that means required a cohort in the house.

"God love us, I hope his lordship didn't have his gold hidden down here, to be stolen out from under our noses!" she exclaimed, and sequestered the coin in the bosom of her dress.

"That's what it is!" Willard said. "His servants have been in and out of this cellar a dozen times, choosing wines for Lord Aiglon. One of them opened that door and went slipping in from the outside so we'd not see him. It's not on our heads, Meg. I'll speak to her ladyship."

"Lock the door first, gudgeon!" she ordered, and he did.

Then we all went back upstairs and Willard went to Rachel. I was sure she would join us to discuss this major event, but she only sent Willard back down with word that she knew nothing about the matter, and if Aiglon was foolish enough to carry such sums about with him and to employ larcenous servants, it had nothing to do with her.

"Why was he talking of selling our house if he was as rich as a nabob?" Meg asked me.

"Maybe he sold it already, and that was the purchase

104

price," Willard suggested, and was roundly condemned for a cloth head.

"We don't know that it was Aiglon's money," I pointed out.

"We know it wasn't mine or yours or Willard's," Meg retorted sharply. "And if it belonged to the mistress, she wouldn't be calmly sitting upstairs reading that everlasting book. She'd be off hollering to the constable."

This irrefutable logic did indeed point back to Aiglon as the possessor of the money. Shiftwell was summoned, and he turned a blank face to us all.

"His lordship did not travel with any large sum of money," he stated firmly. And added, "Quite the contrary," in a way that suggested pockets to let.

"There's a riddle wrapped up in a mystery then," Meg declared, and drew out her coin.

It was newly minted, which set my mind at rest on one bothersome question. When Meg mentioned Rachel reading that "everlasting book," I feared Rachel had outsmarted me and gone on to find some buried treasure after all. But the coin Meg held was not more than a few months old, to judge by its sheen.

I went upstairs to speak to Rachel and found her lying on her bed, though fully dressed. She was too far from the lamp to have been reading.

"Rachel, what should we do about the man in the cellar?" I asked.

"You'd best mention it to Aiglon when he returns."

"It's important enough that we should send someone into town to get him!"

"No, he won't want any publicity," she said. It was unusual that she didn't even bother sitting up to talk to me, but remained lying down.

"Are you not feeling well? Would you like a headache powder?" I asked.

"I'm just a little tired. I haven't been sleeping well. I'm very worried about Aiglon's goings-on here. You know where that money came from, of course?"

"No, I have no idea."

"It's the money he got for selling those arms to the Frenchies. That's why he was careful to hide it in the cellar. And it is also why he wouldn't thank us for raising any alarm at its loss. He can't even report the theft. It serves him right," she said grimly.

"That can't be it, Rachel!" I objected, but I remembered his extraordinary ability with a lie and found myself in great doubt.

We discussed it for a few moments. We were still doing so when Willard knocked at the door and was told to come in.

"There's company downstairs looking for his lordship," Willard said.

"Is it the law?" I asked, my bones turning to ice.

"Oh, no, miss. It's nothing like the law" was Willard's strange reply.

"Well, who is it?" Rachel demanded, finally lifting herself to an upright position.

"He says the name's Sir Edward Retchling, but folks call him Beau. Have you ever heard of him at all?"

"No, but it sounds like a name worth investigating. The Retchlings are more than respectable. We'll be down presently, Willard. Give Sir Edward a glass of wine and make him comfortable," she said.

"He's already given himself a glass," Willard replied, and shuffled out, his poor shoulders stooping.

"Don't speak of the man in the cellar or the satchel of gold in front of Retchling, Constance. Let me talk to Aiglon about it first," Rachel instructed.

She also suggested I make myself presentable, employing her rouge pot if necessary, for I looked like a ghost. The tallow had also stained my gown, so by the time I changed and went below, Sir Edward was comfortably ensconced. His clear, fluting voice struck my ears from halfway down the staircase, but his physical presence was more striking by far. I had never seen such a pretty gentleman.

CHAPTER NINE

SIR EDWARD WAS AT LEAST SIX FEET TALL WITH BROAD shoulders, so it is strange that the overall impression when first laying eyes on him was that he ought, by rights, to be wearing a bonnet. I don't know whether it was his languid, die-away air or his fine-featured face that first put the notion into my head, but, once there, I could hardly look at him without smiling. He had baby blue eyes, heavily fringed, a pouting set of lips, and a weak chin, but to counteract these adornments, he also had a nose of considerable proportions. He arose to make a ludicrously graceful bow when Rachel and I entered. I observed at once that I had another elegant person to contend with. There were no wrinkles in his well-fitted jacket, no tarnish on its large brass buttons, no dust on his boots, no intimation that he had traveled any distance since leaving his dressing room.

"Ladies, your servant," he said, scraping a leg most artfully.

"Sir Edward, I'm Aiglon's cousin, Lady Savage. Allow me to make you welcome at Thornbury," Rachel said, and went on to make me acquainted with him.

We all sat down before the desultory embers in the grate and stared at one another. "I'm afraid Aiglon is out for the evening," Rachel explained. "He may not come home for a few hours. If you are anxious to see him, you'll find him at the White Hart in Folkestone. It's only . . .''

"Your excellent butler was kind enough to tell me so, ma'am. I have taken the liberty of having Shiftwell sent off to fetch him. He should be here soon," Retchling replied.

The casual use of Shiftwell's name, along with the rather encroaching way of using Aiglon's servants, suggested that Sir Edward and Aiglon were close friends. Rachel had soon made inquiries in this direction.

"Bosom bows," he confirmed. "I come with tidings of great joy. You heard of the Kirkwell fracas?"

"Yes," Rachel replied, nose sliding chinward.

"I have the honor to be Aiglon's second in all his duels. I am happy to be able to inform you that your cousin acquitted himself admirably. A good but not fatal hit, and Aiglon was three sheets to the wind at the time, too. But to be defending the honor of a lightskirt! 'Twas farce, not drama. Still, all's well that ends well. The fellow has recovered sufficiently to inflict himself on society once more. I immediately dashed forward to tell Lance."

"He has already heard it," Rachel told him. "Someone else wrote the news to him. You shouldn't have bothered driving so far, Sir Edward."

"I spare no exertion where my true friends are concerned," he professed nobly, then ran on as frankly as if he sat alone. "I wonder if Lance will know I knew Riddell wrote. I must come up with a better excuse, as that one has evaporated like dew in the morning sun."

"Why don't you tell him the *reason* instead?" Rachel suggested, and her curious glance added that she wouldn't mind hearing it herself.

"One will end up doing so in the end. Pockets to let," he mentioned. "Bailiff roosting at Watley Hall—my own country place. He's counting the silver to see I don't pawn or sell it. Entailed, of course. Still, Lance won't cavil at that. He's in much the same boat himself.''

I had come to accept that Aiglon was an accomplished liar. I now had to swallow either that Retchling was equally accomplished or that Aiglon was, in fact, in the basket. And if he had lied to me about that, what confidence could be placed on any of his other explanations? Most of all, I was chagrined to hear that the duel had involved a light-skirt, and that it was, apparently, one of a series of such disgraceful exhibitions. He had never denied the duel or explained it to me.

''You have come to stay a while then, Sir Edward?'' Rachel asked, trying to conceal the wrath that I knew must be roiling in her breast.

''For a *petit* sojourn by the sea, but I shan't be any trouble to you, Lady Savage. I shall quietly inhabit the library. In my more cerebral or at any rate less physical moments, I enjoy to brush minds with other geniuses.''

''I see,'' Rachel answered, biting back a smile. ''And are you a genius as well, Sir Edward?''

''It troubles my modesty to say so, but I have at last submitted to popular clamor and acknowledge it. My collection of *Pensées* was well-received. Rather in the manner of Blaise Pascal, but less theological. Pascal with muscles, the critics said. Rather clever of them. I slipped the phrase to Hazlitt but can't claim credit for the *bon mot* that was circulating at court. 'Twas said I set Pascal ablaze. Blaise Pascal, you see. A pun. A lowly joke, and not even my own.''

Sir Edward soon admitted that he was feeling peckish, so Rachel ordered him some cold food, and no sooner was it consumed than Aiglon arrived.

Sir Edward jumped up from his chair, where he had been eating with a plate on his lap. ''Lance, dear boy, what a world of good it does these tired eyes to see you!'' he exclaimed, and paced forward to shake Aiglon's hand.

I compared the two, marveling that despite the similarity in build, they looked so very different. Retchling was perhaps eight or ten years older, but the greater disparity was in their air. Retchling was an affected fop, and it seemed strange to me that the pair could be intimate friends.

''What a surprise, R—''

''No, don't call me Retchling!'' Sir Edward interrupted, shaking a playful finger under his host's nose. ''It is the style since your departure to call me Beau. I am locked in mortal combat with Brummell for the title of greatest dandy in all of England. Tell me truthfully, now, Lance, what think you of this jacket?'' he asked, performing a pirouette for Aiglon's benefit. ''It may not sit quite so well between the shoulder blades as Brummell's, but it shows to better advantage in the sleeves, don't you agree?''

''It is no worse than Brummell's,'' Aiglon decided after careful consideration. Retchling looked quite crushed. I thought Aiglon could have added one harmless little lie to his total since it was obviously a matter of such importance to his friend.

''Ah, to the quick! You strike me to the quick,'' Retchling said sadly.

''What calamity has forced you beyond London, Beau?'' Aiglon asked, walking in and taking a seat. Perhaps he read the eagerness in my face, for he sat beside me. I was on thorns to tell him of my experience in the cellar and to learn if he was involved.

''My old chronic complaint,'' Retchling admitted. His financial troubles were apparently well-enough known that no further elucidation was required. ''But I'm not here to beg, old bean. Never fear it. I know you are not well-to-grass yourself at the moment. I am almost on the point of taking your advice and marrying myself a plump heiress.

111

Plump in the pocket, I mean. *Ça va sans dire*. I could never tolerate a squabby woman.'' He looked hopefully toward myself at this speech. Aiglon just shook his head to denote my lack of funds. Next Rachel was examined as a possible bride. She was, I think, two or three years older than Retchling, but in the dim lamplight she passed for a little younger.

Her quick eyes didn't miss a move. I was surprised to see a little look of pleasure on her lean countenance. I had never thought of Rachel as being at all interested in marriage, perhaps because we met so few eligible gentlemen at Thornbury. She immediately turned her attention to Retchling and began offering him wine and plum cake, both of which he accepted.

While this was going forth, I spoke in low tones to Aiglon, informing him what had happened during his absence.

''Was it *your* money?'' I asked fearfully. He hadn't appeared the least dismayed to learn that it was gone, so I was inclined to think he knew nothing about it.

I must have spoken the word *money* louder than I intended, for suddenly both Retchling and Rachel were looking at me, their faces alive with curiosity.

''No!'' Aiglon answered, greatly surprised.

Retchling spoke up then, before I could ask more questions. ''Did I tell you I have a few messages for you, Lance? Lord Tate has written about buying your grays. I indicated a keen lack of interest on your part, to drive up the price. Lady Alice insists you return for her ball, and Taffy Wade says he requests the return with interest of the loan he made you last July. Here, the demmed papers are ruining the set of my jacket.''

He arose and handed a few letters to Aiglon, who pocketed them without looking at them. I was somewhat surprised when Aiglon mentioned what I had been at pains to keep private.

"What's this about some man in the cellar, Rachel?" he asked, right in front of Retchling.

"Ask Constance. She is the one who saw him."

I told my story once more. It attracted its proper share of interest and concern. Aiglon and Retchling asked a million questions. Wasn't I hurt? Did he strike me? Aiglon asked these with enough anxiety to please me.

"Oh, I say, no gentleman would strike a lady!" Retchling objected.

"No gentleman would be lurking about in the cellar," Rachel mentioned.

" 'Twould be odd, but I don't see that it would be bad ton," Retchling told her after careful consideration.

"We'd best have a look," Aiglon decided, and we all trooped down to the kitchen after him, carrying tapers and lamps to light our way.

"You won't find nothing," Meg told us. "Me and Willard have been over the cave with a fine-tooth comb, and he hasn't left a sign, not so much as a hair of his head or the mark of his boot."

She was right. There was nothing to give any indication who had been there or what he had done with the gold. We returned abovestairs to discuss how the intruder had gotten into the cellar. Though Aiglon insisted his servants were a bunch of saints, we considered them the culprits, and he agreed to question them.

"We'll have a look about outside tomorrow," Retchling remarked, but only to pacify Rachel and myself. "And now, dear boy, if you'd be kind enough to point my nose in the proper direction, I shall betake myself to bed."

Rachel had passed Willard the word to make one of the guest rooms ready, and she took Retchling up herself, which left me with a moment of privacy with Aiglon. There were half a dozen things I wanted to talk to him about. The duel over a lightskirt, the note from Lady Alice bidding him to her ball, just what he had accomplished in Folkestone before being called home, and was he or was he not short of money—these were a few that rose to mind. But, of course, it was of the intruder that he spoke first.

"Why didn't you send word to me at the inn as soon as it happened?" he demanded, rather sharply.

"In the first place, I didn't think you were really at the inn!" I replied in the same explosive way.

"I was, and the fact that I'm stone-cold sober should alleviate your fears that I overindulge while there," he pointed out.

"Rachel didn't think you'd want the story about the gold to be circulated publicly."

"Why not?"

"Because she thinks it's yours, money you got for selling secrets to the French," I answered unhesitatingly.

His lips pinched into a thin line. "You share this suspicion, I assume?"

"I don't see why else so much money would be in your cellar."

"You don't even know that the black bag *did* contain money! One guinea rolled across the floor. The man could have dropped it out of his hand."

"It sounded like money. It felt like money. If it was only some surgeon's tools or something harmless, why did he scare me? I would never have seen him if he hadn't growled and let me know he was there. It was as dark as night. He just wanted to get rid of me so that he could pick up his money and run away. You seemed to have gotten home from the White Hart in very good time, Aiglon," I mentioned. "And sober, too. Are you sure you were ever there at all?"

"Now you're saying *I* was the man in the cellar, frightening you!" he exclaimed. His expression was one of absolute astonishment. It almost absolved him as the culprit.

"For that matter, it could have been Beau Retchling," I said then, thinking aloud.

"Yes, and it could have been an active imagination," he retaliated.

"Meg has the guinea to prove it," I reminded him.

"So she has. I forgot that. You know, it's possible one of the servants is working with the Gentlemen. Mickey may have stashed his purchase money here."

"No, they land at the Romney Marsh, miles away. Why would he leave it here in Rachel's—your cellar."

"I don't know," he admitted. "But I'm glad Retchling is here. We'll mount a guard for the next few nights to see if our intruder returns."

"He wouldn't be fool enough to return to the same spot! If he's using Thornbury at all, he'd go somewhere else. To the stables or . . . I don't know. The chapel, perhaps." Any mention of the chapel was bound to remind me of Rachel. She admitted she had been there looking for treasure.

Had she found it? Not old treasure, but new. Why had she suddenly offered to show me the ancient book? Why had she admitted she'd been searching for gold chalices and monstrances? What had she learned that night she went down to the chapel in the rain? The only person I could think of in the whole neighborhood who had any reason to lug around a bag of gold was Mickey Dougherty. He'd have a lot of cash when he sold his brandy to whomever he sold it to, and he'd also have it when he had to pay off his Gentlemen. Leaving it at Lord Ware's house might not appeal to him. The old lord was a bit high in the instep.

Had Rachel come upon him hiding his gold somewhere in the old ruined chapel? She wouldn't give a tinker's curse that he was doing it, but she would demand a share of the profit. She'd told me more than once to keep Aiglon away from that particular spot. Perhaps she was afraid we'd discover Mick's secret. He'd be forced to find another hiding place, and she'd lose her cut of the profit. Perhaps it was Rachel herself who unlocked the cellar door for Mick, allowing him to use the cellar while Aiglon was here, as the chapel had proved of such interest to her cousin. That would explain why she wasn't unduly concerned about our intruder and why she hadn't sent for Aiglon at the inn.

"What is it? You've thought of something," Aiglon said, peering closely at me. I wanted time to give my thoughts further study before revealing them to anyone.

Before he had time to quiz me, I diverted attack by launching an offensive of my own. "Sir Edward has been giving us a very odd idea of your character, Aiglon. He mentioned the reason for the duel with Kirkwell . . ."

"The shaved cards weren't mine, I assure you."

"Was the lightskirt yours? He was naive enough to tell us the *truth*, you see."

He scowled and muttered something into his collar. "What else did he tell you?"

"That he is *always* your second. That he knows better than to try to borrow money from you, as you are out of pocket. I believe he substantiated all the wicked things one hears of you except the one that you sold arms to the French."

He took a deep, meditative breath and launched into a disjointed explanation. "The fact is, Constance, I've been a little less than frank with you."

"No, Aiglon, you have been a *great deal* less than frank!"

"R-Retchling knows why I came down here. He was trying to do me a favor by blackening my character, to make it more likely that any disreputable person looking for a partner would approach me. He had no way of knowing I had revealed the truth to you. I shall tell him so tonight, but, for the present, don't tell Rachel. She sees

116

more of Dougherty than she tells us, and I don't entirely trust *him* by any means. Did you know he was to call this afternoon while we were out? Shiftwell informed me.''

''No!'' I gasped, and took it for confirmation of my suspicions regarding who was in the cellar. It would be just like Mickey not to strike a lady, only to frighten her with a growl. I could almost convince myself that I had recognized an Irish brogue in that sound.

''I thought it might surprise you. I hadn't expected it to have this strong an impact!'' Aiglon exclaimed. ''Do you know what's going on between them, Constance?''

''No!'' I answered, and deemed it wise to retire then, before he weaseled it out of me. ''We'll talk about it in the morning. I'm fatigued after the exertions of this night. As though a bogeyman in the cellar weren't enough, we have to be visited by a self-proclaimed genius as well.''

''Has Beau been telling you about his muscular *Pensées*?'' he asked, smiling. ''No further excuses are needed to retire, Constance. I appreciate the tiring effect of those epigrams. They've sent me to bed with a Blaise-ing headache more than once. Too tired for a pun? Never mind, it will come to you soon.''

''Retchling beat you to that particular pun, Aiglon.''

''Ah, yes, he set Pascal a-Blaise for you, did he?''

''You two must be very close. You know each other's very thoughts. I wouldn't dream of saying *pensées*,'' I added.

''We see each other every day. Several times a day.''

''The best mirror, folks say, is an old friend. I hadn't seen that much reflection of you in Retchling.''

''Don't judge him too harshly. Beau's not exactly as he seems on first acquaintance.''

''Somehow that doesn't surprise me. Nothing to do with you is as it seems,'' I answered. Such a shifting image of

Aiglon was reeling about in my head, I didn't know whether I was looking at a traitor or a lover.

"One thing is, Constance," he said, and leaned his head down to kiss my cheek. "That doesn't change. And neither do our plans for tomorrow's picnic. We'll lock Beau up in the library to flirt with Homer and Virgil, and go gallivanting off into the wilds."

I had to steel myself against this insidious promise and the soft light that shone in Aiglon's eyes. "You have your cousin Rachel's way of getting the most feathers from the goose with the least hissing, but pray don't mistake me for a peagoose, Aiglon."

"You disappoint me, Constance! A peagoose is exactly what a peacock like myself was hoping for. Mind you, I prefer your feathers intact," he added softly, with one finger stroking my cheek till I twitched away.

He patted his pocket. I took the notion that he was eager to be reading his correspondence and said good night.

I had a great deal to think about before I went to sleep. I didn't much care for Aiglon's friend and wondered if Beau was one of the ones who had been leading Aiglon into bad conduct. Or had the whole charge of wrong conduct been claimed a lie? The letter and the drinking were only inventions to let him come here in disgrace, but what of the duel? He hadn't denied that. Yet, as I considered matters, I remembered the duel hinged on his having been drunk for two days. Doubts gnawed at the edges of my happiness, and I tried to calm them. All young bucks drank a little more than they should. They all gambled, too. Probably Aiglon's involvement in these pastimes seemed normal to him.

In any case, his character in London couldn't be totally ruined if a Lady Alice was bidding him to her ball. Then I had to allot a few moments to worrying over Lady Alice and how much competition she might be. Last of all, I worried about Rachel, wondering if she had inveigled her way into the smuggling ring. I am sorry to say that I didn't put such a thing an inch past her. It wouldn't have surprised me much if she ended up taking a more active role.

Aiglon's visit had brought more excitement to Thornbury than I had ever anticipated, and more worries. The little matter of the unbuilt dovecote and new-old carpets and curtains had ceased to matter. They shrank to peccadilloes in light of such goings-on as smuggling and treason.

CHAPTER TEN

IT WAS NEXT TO IMPOSSIBLE TO SLEEP WITH SUCH A PLETHora of questions. It seemed the whole house was restless that night. I never did hear Aiglon come upstairs. I heard Rachel moving about in her room, then heard the bed squawk when she finally placed herself on it not too long before midnight. I heard someone—Willard, to judge by the dragging steps—traverse the upstairs corridor with some attempt at silence. First I became curious, then thirsty, and after half an hour of lying in my bed thinking perfectly jumbled thoughts, I convinced myself that I was hungry. I arose, wrapped my dressing gown around me, and opened the door. There was utter darkness all around. No light came up from below, and I tiptoed quietly along the hall and down the stairs to go to the kitchen.

Below the kitchen door, a crack of light showed that someone was still up and about. I listened for a moment, telling myself that if it was Aiglon and/or Retchling, I would retire without entering. The only voice I heard was Rachel's, but as she was demanding service, obviously Willard was with her.

"Not too hot, and not too much cocoa. Just enough to flavor the milk," she said.

I welcomed the opportunity to talk to her and pushed the

door open. Rachel jumped a foot from her chair and stared at me as though I were a ghost.

"What are you doing creeping about the house like a thief in the night?" she demanded sharply.

"I couldn't sleep. I wouldn't mind some of that cocoa, too, Willard." I went to the table and sat down beside her.

Rachel was in her dressing gown, like myself. There was nothing to suggest that she'd been out of the house, which was my first suspicion.

"Sleep! Hah! Who can sleep with thieves and murderers for all we know under the roof?" she demanded, pulling her gown more closely over her shoulders.

"Are you talking about the man I saw in the cellar or Aiglon?" I asked.

"The two are not necessarily mutually exclusive," she informed me, nodding her head sagely. "Though actually I don't think it was Aiglon in the cellar. I've been giving this matter a good deal of thought, Constance. It wasn't half an hour after you sounded the alarm that Retchling came pounding on the door. Who is to say it wasn't Retchling you saw downstairs?"

I considered this for a moment and could offer no proof that it hadn't been Beau. "If it was him, I don't know where he could have gotten the bag of money" was all I had to say.

Willard served us cocoa and busied himself at the sink, tidying up, but with his ears stretched. "He brought it from London where he's been hiding it for Aiglon, so the Runners or the army or whoever investigates such things wouldn't find it when they searched his house," she explained.

"No, it can't be that. If Retchling brought it, it's his own money," I insisted.

"Where would that rattle get two pennies to rub together? Both he and Aiglon have got themselves in the suds, I tell you, and have taken to a life of crime.''

"Oh, Rachel, you're imagining things,'' I parried.

"Am I imagining that the pair of them are down at the ruined chapel this instant, having a secret rendezvous with Mickey Dougherty?'' she asked.

I felt a wave of something very like nausea. I looked at Willard, and he nodded his head in confirmation. "What on earth were you doing out at this hour?'' I asked him.

"I set him to follow the pair of them when they left the house half an hour ago,'' Rachel told me. "And they've got the satchel of money with them,'' she added importantly.

I refused to look truth in the face. "Maybe it only has to do with smuggling,'' I suggested, but only halfheartedly. "Mickey *did* offer to take Aiglon to France when his *Mermaid* arrives.''

"And how, I ask you, would that involve Aiglon's giving Mickey a bag of gold? They're paying that scoundrel off to help them steal the new shipment and sell it to the Frenchies,'' she declared firmly. "Retchling brought a part of the money from the first lot down to arrange the theft of the second. We'll never be able to hold up our heads again. We've got to find out when the arms are arriving, Constance, and hold Retchling and Aiglon in the cellar, in chains if necessary, till the army has safely got its guns.''

I could only stare at such an outrageous scheme, and Rachel spoke on, lest I argue. "Pray don't tell me it is my duty to report them. It is a Howell's first duty to protect the family name. And you have got to help me. It's your duty as an Englishwoman.''

"What about his servants? You said they offered to help?'' I reminded her.

"They lied,'' she said bluntly. "Aiglon put them up to

122

it. They know perfectly well what is going on and are in on it. Aiglon's groom reported to me this very evening that his lordship was at the inn, and Willard overheard Aiglon talking to Retchling about Madame Bieler. What was it he said, Willard?'' she asked, looking toward the table.

Willard screwed up his face with the effort to recall the speech verbatim, and I listened in much the same way. ''He said: 'I pulled the better duty this time, my lad. I enjoyed a delightful evening with Madame, while you . . .' Then the wind came up, and I couldn't hear the rest, but they all laughed heartily. Except for Dougherty. He gave them a bit of a dressing-down, being as how he's sweet on Madame himself.''

''Things have come to a fine pass when it takes an Irish smuggler to bring two English gentlemen to propriety!'' Rachel declared.

''You're on terms with Dougherty, Rachel. Can't you find out what's going on?'' I suggested. My voice took on a new, harder timbre. There was no longer any point in pretending Aiglon wasn't as black as the ace of spades. He was a confirmed villain, and I quite agreed with Rachel that it was our duty to outwit him. Unlike Rachel, however, I did not put the illustrious name of Howell before the safety of England. If we couldn't contrive the matter ourselves, I would enlist Captain Cokewell and Lord Ware and anyone else I could think of to help us.

''I, on terms with Mick Dougherty?'' she asked, her eyebrows lifting up to her hair. ''Like the rest of the world, I speak to him because of his mother. I don't know what you imply by the word 'on terms,' Constance, but if you're suggesting anything more than common civility, I must ask you to explain yourself.''

There's no point arguing with Rachel when she runs to high ground. Pressing the matter would only freeze her up like a pond in winter, and that would do no good.

"Well, what do you suggest we do?" I asked.

"My groom has orders to dog every step Aiglon takes, unless either you or I are with him. Willard sent him down to the chapel when he returned. The cold was punishing Willard's back, and he couldn't stay. As you know, our groom has a brother. When Jeremy comes back from the chapel, I'll send him home to enlist Jake's help as well. Between the two of them, they'll harry Aiglon and Dougherty till we discover who they're dealing with. As to Retchling, I believe he's only a tool, an errand boy. Mind you, we'll watch him as much as possible, too."

While we were still discussing our strategy, Jeremy came bustling in at the back door. Jeremy Chubb was a husky young fellow of nineteen or twenty, redheaded, capable, and handy with his fists. "They're acoming home, milady. Mick took the bag of gold home with him. From what was said, it seems the night after tomorrow is when they make their move."

"You see!" Rachel crowed, smiling with success. "It is only for two days, Constance." Then she turned her attention back to Jeremy. "Could you learn anything of when and where the arms will be stolen?"

"They was talking about boats, milady. That's all I could make out. Mickey, he seemed to think wagons would be used, but his lordship, he said that was all a ruse."

The accomplished liar had struck again, leading Cokewell to believe the arms would come by land! I was more determined than ever to stop him. I'd see Aiglon's lying mouth begging for mercy before I was through.

"Are they on foot or mounted?" Rachel asked.

"All the nags is in the stable," Jeremy answered.

"Excellent. Well, then, we had best disperse, had we not? We wouldn't want the gentlemen to begin wondering what we're all doing gathered around the table at one o'clock in the morning."

This suggestion was followed with all haste. Jeremy was out the door, Rachel and I grabbed our cocoa and ran for the stairs, while Willard extinguished the candle and shuffled off to his room just above the kitchen.

Rachel stopped me at her door. "One of us ought, by rights, to listen at the door and hear what Aiglon and Retchling have to say," she informed me. "They'll stay in the kitchen, for privacy's sake, I should think. If you station yourself just this side of the door, Constance, you shouldn't have any trouble overhearing them. Run along now, and you'll be there before they come in."

There had never been any doubt in mind which of us would be chosen for the job, but I wasn't reluctant. I handed her my cup and ran back downstairs to take up my post. I didn't have to wait long before the back door opened and steps were heard.

I listened for voices while they went about the business of lighting candles and was very much surprised to hear one I had never heard before. It wasn't Retchling's high, fluting tone or Aiglon's deeper one, but something in between. I put my eye to the crack in the door and saw that it was Retchling who spoke but not in Retchling's voice.

"How's the cellar here for a decent wine?" he asked.

"You should know, Beau!" Aiglon answered, laughing. This sounded mighty like a hint that Retchling had already been in our cellar, and it was soon confirmed.

"I was too busy scaring the pretty young lady to read labels," he answered lightly, and looked around for the cellar door.

"You're sure she didn't recognize you?" Aiglon asked.

"She'd have said something if she had. The only look on her face when I went into my Retchling act was one of astonishment. Pity she thinks me an idiot," he added.

"Count your blessings. She thinks *I* am a traitor," Aiglon replied.

It is a sad comment on my vanity that I experienced some pleasure at hearing myself discussed in this flattering way. With such interesting comments being exchanged, however, I soon had more important thoughts. "She thinks I am a traitor." Surely there was some implication in this that he was *not* a traitor?

"I should bloody hope so!" said the man who was not Retchling, but who had borrowed his name, just before he went downstairs for the wine.

Aiglon was writing something on a piece of paper. When the man whom I shall continue to call Retchling, for want of a better name, returned, he held two dusty bottles in his hands.

They opened them and wasted a few moments in proclaiming the claret "beautifully sound." Each took his own bottle and drank from it without benefit of a glass.

"Can we count on Dougherty, do you think?" Retchling asked.

"With his neck in a noose and his foot on a patch of ice, we can count on him," Aiglon answered.

"I prefer voluntary cooperation to press-gang tactics myself. Who's to say he won't take the money and run?" Retchling queried.

"He won't run, Beau. I've kept an ace up my sleeve," Aiglon answered, and laughed sardonically. "There are some things money can't buy. Fortunately for us, Mickey isn't one of them. I don't know who is the greater scoundrel, Cousin Rachel or Mickey Dougherty."

Retchling made a *tsk*ing sound in Rachel's defense. "A fine lady, she struck me. I'm just surprised she keeps herself stuck away here at Thornbury," he said.

"She'd live in a bog if it were rent free. What I can't understand is why Miss Pethel stays here with her."

"Not exactly a member of the nubility, old bean. Mean to say, pretty and all that, but . . ."

"Is that a slur on the lady's age or lack of a title?" Aiglon asked, sharply enough to please me.

"Oh, dear, I come to see no slur on anything but her domicile is acceptable. Fine, she is an Incomparable. Shall I call her a duchess as well? Or is it a *countess* you plan to make her?" Retchling asked. His voice, ironic and unpleasant, gave me an idea of how he would look as he said this.

"You're an ass, Beau. Pray don't become an egregious ass or I shall be tempted to dispense with your services."

"My regular services, milord, or these highly irregular ones you are currently involving me in? If the F.O. had the least notion what you're doing down here, they'd have your head on a platter."

All the assurance of "She thinks me a traitor" was blown away by this last speech. The Foreign Office *wasn't* sponsoring this mission then, as I had begun to hope. And on top of that disappointment, Aiglon had called his friend an ass for hinting at a possible marriage to me.

"Both," Aiglon said. They each took another drink of wine and sat in silence for a moment.

"You know what to do tomorrow?" Aiglon asked a moment later.

Retchling's voice still bore traces of having taken offense. "Have you ever found me to fail you in the past?"

"Not fail, precisely, Beau, but you have a somewhat troublesome way of succeeding. I'm referring to letting that bag of golden boys in the cellar be seen. I hope the ladies don't take it into their heads to do something stupid."

"Surely the Incomparable Miss Pethel is above stupidity?" Beau asked, still in his ironic vein.

"I never said she was clever, Beau. Just pretty."

I weighed this piece of condescension and found it wanting. Not clever? We'd see about that!

"And what will you be doing while I find a suitable ship

for hauling the guns?'' Retchling asked. The very blood in my veins curdled. Why did they have to find a ship for hauling guns unless they meant to ship them to France? The army would have its own ship if the guns were to come down to Folkestone from Bristol by water.

"I'll be having a tête-à-tête with the enchanting Madame Bieler,'' Aiglon replied, with more satisfaction than I liked.

"Another Incomparable!'' Retchling exclaimed.

"I seem to be drawing good luck this time,'' Aiglon agreed blandly.

"Yes, indeed. You were fortunate to come across such a woman—outside of a brothel, I mean.''

"The stream of gentlemen who enter her door usually leave with a bag under their arms. She isn't selling anything but brandy and a little silk. It's small-town gossip that has added that other aura to her. She's not a loose or vulgar woman. In fact, Mickey assures me her lineage is old and noble,'' Aiglon answered haughtily.

"I looked into it in London, as you requested, milord. Her ancient lineage can be traced back as far as the orphanage, where her mother dumped her. The orphanage is old and has a noble patroness. That's closer to the truth than you usually find Dougherty straying, I fancy, from what I've seen of the bleater.''

"You actually learned something about her?'' Aiglon asked, surprised. "I hardly thought it worthwhile to have you check up. What do they know of her there other than her lack of parents?''

"The chief clerk at the F.O. has a list of Frenchmen living in England who are considered not precisely guilty but suspicious. When the arms shipment lost en route to Folkestone was looked into, Madame's name was added to the list. It was learned that she has invested more money than her legitimate trade could account for in real estate in Ireland. It was done over several years, however, and we assumed she either dealt with the French or had a rich patron.''

''I fancy Mickey has a few sheckles stashed away, but I can't see him buying land in Madame's name. No reason not to buy it in his own,'' Aiglon said.

''As she is apparently selling nothing but brandy and a little silk, and only entertaining Mr. Dougherty for money, we seem to be wending our way to the conclusion that she deals in something else besides. Her Irish holdings are considerable—more than retailing a spot of brandy could account for. No, my friend, Madame is in deeper than that. She'll make an interesting partner in crime, *n'est-ce pas*?''

That last was added in a playful way. But still it was added. Aiglon and Retchling were involved in something the government wouldn't countenance. Whether they did it for money or to clear any stain on Aiglon's character, I had no way of knowing. It was disturbing enough that they meant to involve themselves with Madame Bieler in some havey-cavey business, whatever the cause. I listened sharply for Aiglon's answer.

''A dangerous one, Beau. I *do* enjoy tangling with a dangerous woman,'' he said.

I felt a nearly uncontrollable urge to rush in and chastise him.

''You don't have to tell me. I know it well,'' Retchling said. His weary voice implied that such entanglements were frequent enough to have become a bore. ''I'm about ready for the goose feathers. How about you?''

''More than ready.''

There was the sound of scuffling feet as they stood up. I ran up the stairs before they could open the door and discover me with my ear to the keyhole.

Rachel's door opened a crack, and I fled into her room. ''What did you learn?'' she asked eagerly.

"They're going to hire a boat and get hold of the arms somehow. Mickey and Madame Bieler are in on it as well."

"Forewarned is forearmed," she announced, her face glowing with triumph. "Well done, Constance. You can leave the matter in my hands. Better get along to bed now. I'll plan our strategy. Day after tomorrow, Jeremy said. It won't be long till they're gone, and we'll have the place to ourselves again to . . . to get back to normal," she finished, but her eyes bore a shifty look that I couldn't account for.

The bag of gold was explained in a way that didn't involve Rachel with Mickey and his smuggling. But still I felt she was mixed up with him in something. She was in a pelter to push me out the door before Aiglon and Retchling mounted the stairs, and I went without protest.

I tried to make some sense out of all the strange things I had heard and overheard, but it seemed the more I learned, the less I could figure out. There were intrigues here within schemes, like a Chinese puzzle. "She thinks me a traitor" didn't jibe with the F.O. having Aiglon's head on a platter. Rachel's shifty-eyed eagerness to have Aiglon gone from Thornbury didn't jibe with her not being involved in some wicked and probably highly profitable scheme. It *must* include Mickey, or why was she suddenly seeing him so often? Ordering a ship didn't jibe with anything but sneaking the arms off to France. How were all these skeins to be untangled in the two days before Aiglon and Retchling meant to make their move?

The one bright strand in the knot, Aiglon's defense of my attractiveness, was considerably dimmed by his admiration of Madame Bieler. I wondered if it were at all possible that this dainty, porcelain lady actually led a life of crime on the side. It seemed much more probable that Mickey had pulled her into his wickedness. So much going on under my nose and I unaware of it, as Rachel had said.

Mickey's affair with Madame didn't surprise me much, but that he might be serious about her came as a shock. Lord Ware, and even his own mother, would disown him.

And just before I finally dozed off, I found a moment to wonder who Beau Retchling really was. Aiglon called him Beau, even when they were alone. Was it possibly the great Beau Brummell who had come amongst us? But, no, Aiglon spoke to him as one speaks to an employee. Riddell was the first name that popped into my mind. Aiglon had mentioned Riddell's coming the very night he arrived. Hadn't there been some stammering over his R's, too, a few times? I seemed to remember hearing him say "R-Retchling." But why would Riddell come incognito? It was too much to conjure with, and at last I slept.

CHAPTER ELEVEN

IN THE MORNING, I WAS CURIOUS TO LEARN WHETHER HIS picnic with me or his visit to Madame Bieler would be the first item on Aiglon's agenda. As things turned out, a haircut took precedence over both. Aiglon and Retchling both jogged into Folkestone, with Jeremy skulking behind them. When Jeremy reported to Rachel later, the only item of any interest whatsoever was that Mickey Dougherty had also gone for a haircut. Obviously it had been prearranged, but Jeremy wasn't artful enough to discover any manner in which he could overhear their conversation from outside the window. They had talked "thirteen to the dozen" for half an hour, and not a single word of it all was brought home to us!

"They've arranged the whole thing, Rachel, and we are none the wiser," I pointed out.

"Arranging is one thing; doing is another" was her elucidating comment.

The weather was not conducive to a picnic. I was sure it would be proferred as an excuse to cancel or, at least, to delay my outing with Aiglon, but it was no such a thing. It only changed the nature of the trip. We were to go for a drive in his closed carriage. It was agreed that I was to monitor any suspicious actions, leaving Jake and Jeremy free to follow Mickey and Retchling.

I suggested a drive to Dover for our destination as we had already been to Folkestone once.

"We'll do that another time, if you don't mind," Aiglon countered. "I have a little business in Folkestone, which I hope to mix with the pleasure of this outing."

"You were there this morning. Why didn't you tend to your business then?" I asked, but I was interested to learn what business he might have in mind all the same. "Has it something to do with the *Mermaid*?"

"No, it's only a bit of shopping."

"Dover's shops are as fine."

"I daresay what I want is equally available in Dover, but I don't know the shops there. I know exactly where to find good silks in Folkestone. They're difficult to get a hold of in London, you know. I want to surprise Mama by bringing her a few ells," he explained. His face was as innocent as a newborn babe's. A pair of guileless eyes were turned to me.

"I can't think you'll object," he continued blandly. "Most ladies of my acquaintance consider it an accomplishment when they can persuade their gallant to go on the strut with them. Till now I have been immovable in my resistance. But you can talk me into anything, Constance."

"Without even trying!" I said sharply, for I was not pleased to share my bit of time with Aiglon with his other flirt.

He turned his laughing eyes on me and replied, "Don't think I haven't noticed your lack of effort to lead me. And don't think it hasn't been appreciated, too, but there comes a time, you know, when a little proprietary interest from a lady is not taken amiss."

I had to remind myself that Retchling was termed an ass

for suggesting Aiglon's interest in me might be serious. This sort of conversation had no excuse except "honorable intentions" on the gentleman's part. "I try to restrain myself from displaying any proprietary interest in things that aren't my property," I replied.

"Strange how little of Cousin Rachel's ways have rubbed off on you. I've noticed it more than once. The crystal pendants would look better on you than on her, too," he added, using this speech as an excuse to scrutinize my face in a frank way that was extremely disconcerting. "Don't feel obliged to restrain yourself quite so hard, my flower," he added, taking my hand in his.

This was fairly uncomfortable, for we sat on opposite benches, and before long Aiglon used it as an excuse to move over to my seat. I promptly turned my head to look at the scenery, as though unaware that my fingers were firmly clutched in his. The sea was a cold, green-gray sheet of rumpled metal, dotted with dark splotches of boats, above which sails ballooned in the wind. It was pretty, but could hardly claim more than a few minutes of observation. Next I looked out the other window, where hillocks rose up from the coast road. The horizon was interrupted here and there by the Martello towers and furze stacks.

Suddenly I felt Aiglon lurch forward and followed the line of his gaze. A man was galloping across the hills, but this was hardly unusual enough to have caused his lurch. The guards were changed at regular intervals. Soon I noticed that a second mounted figure dogged the first, following behind him, but careful not to be seen. He would change his course to keep himself behind a tree or a furze stack.

I think it was the first rider whom Aiglon recognized. I soon discerned the shape of Jeremy in the follower and deduced that Retchling was the followee. Without a word, Aiglon reached into the side pocket of the carriage and pulled out a telescope. He knelt on the floor at the window, adjusted it to his eye, and stared at the riders for about a minute.

It was hard to keep up any appearance of unconcern, but I tried. "What is it, Aiglon?" I asked in a casual way.

"I don't know. Someone's following that man up there. I wonder if he plans to do him a mischief. He has a secretive air about him."

"In broad daylight? I shouldn't think so." I laughed.

"But look at the way he goes on, dodging behind stacks, always keeping out of sight!" he insisted. "Here, you have a look. You might recognize the man following. I think that's Retchling he's after."

I put the glass to my eye and soon confirmed my suspicions. As Aiglon hadn't recognized Jeremy, however, I had no notion of giving him away. "Yes, it looks like Retchling, all right. What do you suppose he's doing up there? Look, he's stopped to talk to the guards at the tower!"

Aiglon lifted the glass from my fingers and confirmed this news. Jeremy's orders were to remain unseen, so he cantered on. He would take up the chase when Retchling moved on, but his not stopping seemed to ease Aiglon's fears.

"Any visitor to the coast at this time takes an interest in the preparations to thwart Napoleon," Aiglon answered.

"Most do, but somehow I had the impression your genius friend meant to spend his days in the library. Was that not what he said?"

"He's just taking a breath of air," Aiglon decided, and went on to distract me with the most foolish conversation about the doings of the ton in London. I listened with apparent interest, but I didn't forget Aiglon's worry that someone was following Retchling. Why should it matter a groat if Retchling was only out for a breath of air? Of course, Retchling's duty was really to arrange for a ship. The harbor seemed a more likely place to do it, but that was quite public. It was possible some of the men guarding the stacks might possess a boat, for the fishermen were active in the militia.

When we reached town, Aiglon had the carriage taken to the inn and we alit to walk down to the fishing village. It wasn't necessary for me to direct Aiglon's steps toward Madame's shop. He was perfectly familiar with the route. But before we got there, he said, "Why don't you stroll along and do whatever it is you do when you come to town, Constance, and I'll meet you in, say, a quarter of an hour?"

My suspicions soared to new heights, and I determined that I would accompany him to Madame Bieler's place if I had to break his bones to do it, but first I'd try a polite approach. "I have nothing special to do; I'll be happy to go with you."

"It will be boring for you when you're not buying any-thing from her today," he claimed, pretending it was me he was thinking of. "I'll meet you at the 'everything' store. I know ladies can't come to town without dallying there for an age."

"As it happens, I'm looking for material for a new gown myself. I'll look today and buy another time," I persisted.

His smile was still pleasant but less so than before. "Now that's a pity. I promised my valet I'd pick up some shoe blacking and thought you might get it, while I speak to Madame."

"You should have brought some with you, Aiglon!" I declared. "They don't carry it in Folkestone. Lord Ware is always lamenting the fact. But I'm sure he wouldn't mind letting you have some, if you've run out."

The smile had quite vanished, but frustration hadn't taken over yet. "I expect Retchling has some with him," he said, while pondering his next pretext.

"I'm sure he has. Shall we continue? Madame's shop is just along here—the one with the blue door."

"I know where it is," he said, becoming a bit curt now.

"I wasn't sure you'd recognize it by daylight. You more usually visit Madame in the evening, do you not?" The shorter his temper became, the more I poured the honey on my words.

He made one last effort to ditch me. He looked up and down the street and spotted the used-book shop. "I wonder if they have any copies of *The Anatomie of Melancholy* there. I've been trying to find one this age in London. Would you mind terribly, Constance—"

"They don't have one. I asked just a week ago. Strange how similar our tastes are." I smiled firmly.

"They might have got one in since!"

"There's one in the library at home," I lied hastily, losing track of the discussion but not of my purpose.

"Then why did you want to buy another?"

"Because that one is yours, Aiglon. And you know how reluctant I am to claim what is not mine. But, as you hinted, there comes a time when a lady should stake a proprietary claim on a gentleman. I don't plan to let Madame get you all to herself." I tried a fluttering smile, feeling like a fool the whole while.

I was vastly relieved when Aiglon gave in. His knowing look accepted defeat and acknowledged as well that he had some notion why I was sticking like a burr. "I believe I've met my match in stubbornness," he said, relaxing back into a real smile.

"No, you've met your better, Aiglon. Let's go."

"Onward to the blue door," he agreed, and without further ado, we proceeded to the shop.

Madame's appearance was typically French in style, though above the norm in beauty. She had dark hair, flashing eyes, a nose a trifle pointy for my own taste, and a very winsome smile. It was her figure, however, for which she was more famous. She was on the petite side in height, but full-bosomed, wasp-waisted, and well-dimpled at the elbow. As clothing is her trade, she is always well dressed. That day, she wore an elegant golden gown, got up with a lot of lace and ribbons. Her manner is customarily vivacious, but I found her closer to hysterical that morning. Oh, she was polite enough, but her eyes had a febrile glow, and her white fingers twitched nervously.

"Bonjour, mam'selle, monsieur," she said, curtsying gracefully. She was pretending not to recognize Aiglon by not using his title, but as I was already aware of their acquaintance, that formality soon disappeared.

"Good morning, Madame Bieler," Aiglon said. "I've come about that silk you mentioned the other night."

Madame turned a startled eye at his plain speaking, but I walked over to look at her new bonnets. I picked up a leghorn, for which I had no use in the world, and tried it on at the mirror, to encourage them to speak freely.

"Ah, yes, for the countess," Madame said, and went to lift down an ell of shocking red that no lady his mother's age would be caught dead in.

After that speech, she lowered her voice. I walked away to the farther end of the shop, in hopes that they'd think I wasn't listening. I remained there a moment, picking up a couple of bonnets to try on, and when I returned to the mirror, I could just overhear their words. Madame had become Yvette by that time.

They were still discussing silk. She had Aiglon climbing up on a chair to retrieve a green piece from a top shelf. I began to think the visit was entirely innocent of anything but flirtation, for there was plenty of that going on. Madame had to hold every bolt up to her own face to show him how the color would look "on."

"Marvelous, you bring it to life, but somehow I don't

138

think it would suit Mama quite so well," Aiglon was saying. I recognized his accents as those used for serious flirtation.

"Ah, I bring nothing to life today," she said in doleful tones.

"Why, is something the matter, Yvette?" he asked, concern throbbing in his lying voice.

"A little trouble last night, monsieur. Just shortly after you left, I discovered it."

"What sort of trouble?"

"I was robbed," she told him. Her whisper carried across the room so loudly that I feared they'd realize I could hear it. I took a quick peek at them and saw her gazing up into his face while he gazed back. They weren't aware of anything but each other. It was hard to credit, from his sympathetic face, that less than twelve hours before he'd been discussing her with Retchling in quite a different way.

"How much did you lose?" Aiglon asked.

"I had three hundred pounds in the shop. A whole week's income. And it was higher than usual, too, as I had gotten some fine silks in recently. I don't know what I shall do."

"I wish I could help. You'll think it paltry of me not to offer some assistance, Yvette, but the fact is, I'm just about in the basket myself at the moment. Why, if Mama hadn't given me the money to pay for these silks, I'd have to put them on tick. I wish I knew some way we could both recoup our losses."

From the corner of my eye, I saw Madame's dark head turn slowly in my direction. I opened my reticule and took out my brush to arrange my hair, as though unaware that she was looking at me. The silence in the shop stretched until my nerves were on edge.

"Ah, well," she said in a low voice. "Honest money is

139

hard to make. *C'est dommage*. Now about the green *peau de soie*, Lord Aiglon, do you think the countess would care for it?''

Aiglon bought enormous quantities of silk, which Madame bundled up and said she would have delivered to his carriage at the White Hart right away. Aiglon paid her in cash, and we left, with every polite compliment imaginable on both sides. I was surprised that something more hadn't developed. I was sure Madame would get him out to the back of the shop, away from me, on some pretext or other. I was left to wonder whether my presence had defeated Aiglon's purpose in going or whether his mission had been accomplished.

''Satisfied?'' he asked, taking my arm in his when we walked along the street. I concluded that *he* was. Whatever reason took him to Madame Bieler's, he had achieved his aim.

''If you are,'' I parried.

''Now that's odd. You claimed to be interested in looking at stuff for a gown, but you only tried on *chapeaux*.''

''It was pretty obvious you planned to buy all the silk in the shop, so I looked at bonnets instead. Your mother won't care for that hideous red silk, Aiglon.''

''Oh it's not for Mama!'' he said, and laughed.

''No, I should think not. For a lightskirt is more like it!''

''I thought it would suit you remarkably well, Constance. Have I erred?'' he asked.

''I have no desire or intention of decking myself out as a scarlet woman, and if you ever bothered to look at my gowns, you would know scarlet is not my color.''

''That's true, but Madame didn't have anything in gray.''

I felt his ironical eyes sliding in my direction and ignored them as well as the taunting remark. Instead I dropped a hint to see if he'd tell me about Madame's robbery.

140

"Had Madame anything interesting to say?" I asked.

"When one has a face like Madame's, the most commonplace remarks have a way of becoming interesting. She mentioned someone robbing her."

"You sound as if you don't believe it."

"I don't disbelieve it, but why tell *me*? She took the notion I had money to burn and was only trying her hand at relieving me of a little of it."

"Is that what she was up to, with that story of losing a week's income!" I gasped, astonished at her duplicity.

"What big ears you have, Constance! Your careful perusal of the bonnets made me wonder whether you were executing the proper care for my welfare. I'm relieved to confirm your performance a sham."

"I couldn't help overhearing a few words," I admitted, blushing like a rose. The snort that issued from his lips told me as clearly as words his opinion of that statement.

"Well, why did you go, then, and why were you so eager to rid yourself of me, if you only meant to buy silk and hear that Madame was robbed. Oh, dear!" I gasped.

"Precisely, my dear. I had to hear whether Madame was robbed."

"Was it *her* money in our cellar?"

"Probably."

"Aiglon, she can't make that much in a week! Even a good week, with new silks from France."

"You heard those 'few words,' too, did you?"

I was doing some quick figuring and soon spotted a flaw in Aiglon's glib explanation. "You already *knew* Madame had been robbed. You knew her money was in the cellar. You didn't go to her shop to learn that, Aiglon. You're hiding something from me."

"No, Constance, I am only *trying* to hide something from you. I'm quite sure that before we get home you'll have weaseled every detail from me." He slowed the pace and directed a wickedly suggestive smile at me. "At least you could, if you wanted to," he added. That look was more effective than a gun in silencing any further questions from me.

We went for a walk along the Leas to ensure that Aiglon's parcel had time to reach the carriage. The wind was damp and cool, and the view was not at all pretty on such a cloudy day. There were only a handful of people out walking.

"Strange thing, you know, about gentlemen's boots," Aiglon said, staring at the Hessians of a passing stroller.

"What's strange about them?"

"They look so well polished, considering that there's no boot blacking to be had in Folkestone. Truth is indeed stranger than fiction, especially when you invent it. I'm quite shocked at your mendacity, Constance."

"It wasn't exactly a lie," I equivocated. "You knew I was only funning. You haven't been entirely truthful yourself, Aiglon," I was obliged to remind him.

"There are times, I admit, when a lie is not really a lie," he said.

"When it is told by Lord Aiglon, for example?"

He didn't acknowledge my jibe but only frowned in a meditative way out across the water. "Or even Madame Bieler. She tells a sort of truth, yet she misleads. You know that old gray mare in the stable at Thornbury, Constance . . ."

"Yes, what about it?" I asked, curious to hear how a poor old mare should be involved in this discussion.

His frown turned to a triumphant smile. "Ah, then there *is* a gray mare at Thornbury! I suspected as much. And it was a kind of lie by omission for you not to tell me who was following Retchling."

"You tricked me!" I accused. "You let on you were talking about Madame Bieler!"

"No, no, I was only dealing indirectly. Let's go back to the inn now. I'm eager to read the note Madame will have slipped into the packet of silk. All your morning wasted," he taunted, wagging a finger at me. I was so frustrated I wanted to hit him.

And, to make matters worse, he took the note out right in front of me, read it, and tore it into a hundred pieces, which he threw out the window, to flutter off in the wind.

I was furious by the time Rachel quizzed me about my morning's activities. "What did you learn?" she asked eagerly.

"That your cousin is a devious devil!"

"Good gracious, we already knew that. Retchling has been out scouring around the countryside, discovering exactly where the army has outlooks and what routes are safe for the guns. I believe they are coming by land, Constance, and will be taken away on a ship after Aiglon has stolen them."

"Aiglon knows Retchling was followed. And, by the way, I forgot to tell you last night that Retchling is not Retchling. I think he might be Riddell."

"No!" Her face turned bone-white. "I'm sunk. Oh, Constance, I have this very morning been walking around the house with him, discussing the curtains and everything in the most frank way, never thinking he could possibly know my little tricks. He even asked if there was not a dovecote at Thornbury! Thank God I told him it had been vandalized."

"Well, that's something."

"He was so very attentive, too. He came home half an hour before you and spent the entire time with me, just walking around the place, you know. I took the idea he was rather interested in me. The Retchlings are quite unexceptionable. To think I wasted my time being pleasant to Riddell!''

"But you were always buttering him up," I reminded her.

"Only by letter! I would never be so condescending to him in *person*!'' she replied, shocked at my ignorance.

Her next concern was for Aiglon's shopping. "Did he pick up sone nice silks for Lady Aiglon?'' she asked.

"I doubt if his mama will care for the scarlet. Even the peacock blue and gold silk looked a trifle gaudy to me.''

"Peacock blue! How well that would suit the saloon!'' she exclaimed. "Scarlet—I don't know that I'd care for that, but perhaps in one of the smaller guest rooms . . .''

"There was one other thing, Rachel," I said, and waited for her to return to the present conversation before continuing. "That money in the cellar was stolen from Madame Bieler. It was three hundred pounds.''

"That's impossible. She wouldn't make that much in a year," Rachel objected.

I relayed to her what I had overheard the men discussing the night before, and we talked it over for a while. "So you think Retchling stole the money from Madame Bieler? How would he know she had it?''

"Mickey would know, but I can't see why he'd tell Aiglon or Retchling.''

"He wouldn't. He'd steal it himself,'' Rachel answered. "Ah, I think I have it figured out now, Constance. Madame Bieler is the contact Aiglon used when he stole the first lot of guns. It was she who arranged to get the word to the Isle of Wight. He paid her, and he knew she must have the money somewhere around her place, so he came down here to get it. Yes, that must be it. Whatever happened to honor among thieves?''

"But if Aiglon knew it, why did he go to her shop this morning?''

"Ninnyhammer, he went to find out if she suspected him," she told me.

This was as good an explanation as we could come up with. Retchling *had* had the money in the cellar. He must have stolen it, and he couldn't know it was at Madame's house if Aiglon hadn't told him. Stealing from a Frenchie hadn't quite the aroma of selling guns to them, but it was hardly a feather in Aiglon's cap, either. Every time his behavior was put under examination, some new twist turned up.

I was worried that Mickey Dougherty was in on the whole thing, too, for I wouldn't have trusted that man as far as I could throw an elephant. When I remembered how artfully Aiglon had discovered that Jeremy was the man following Retchling, I feared Rachel and I were dealing with men too sharp for us. We were beyond our depths, and I urged her to call in help.

"We'll wait till Jake returns and tells us what Dougherty was up to," she decided. "If Jake can give us the name of the boat they've hired, it will be very simple, Constance. We only have to have that ship watched and foil their whole scheme. That will be preferable to hauling in the army and the constable and making a great scandal for the family. We'll keep Aiglon's name out of it."

I was going to urge her to talk to him, to talk her cousin out of his plan, whatever it was, but in the end I didn't suggest it at all. Aiglon already knew that we were checking up on him. He knew I wouldn't let him out of my sight in town, and he knew that Rachel had had Retchling followed. He wouldn't be dissuaded, and the better plan seemed to be to deal cautiously. His whole success relied on the ship that was being hired, and the ship was what we had to learn about. Not only whose ship it was, but where it would be lying in wait to receive the stolen cargo. Rachel was right, as usual.

We all had dinner together, and afterward Rachel inquired what plans the men had, for she had to arrange to have them followed. Jake still hadn't returned from duty with Mickey Dougherty. It made a quiet evening when Retchling said he would spend his time in the library and Aiglon, malicious eyes dancing, suggested that he and Rachel have a look at the account books for Thornbury.

I had no desire to audit that argument and went upstairs for the next hour, pitying poor Rachel. Aiglon would make mincemeat of the sham and charade of her bookkeeping. I was quite astonished when she came to my door within thirty minutes, gloating and holding the bundle of scarlet silk.

"I got it out of him!" she crowed. "There's enough here to make us both up a lovely gown after they go on back to London. But it's the gold I have my eye on. If I get the gold, I really *will* put this in the smallest guest room. Unless I can sell it back to Madame Bieler," she added, and walked off, humming, to her own room.

I followed after her. "What are Aiglon and Retchling doing?"

"Having a glass of wine. Aiglon asked if you were going belowstairs again."

"Someone had best keep an eye on them," I said, which gave me an excellent excuse to do what I wanted to do without giving Rachel the idea I was tossing my bonnet at her cousin.

CHAPTER TWELVE

THERE WAS NO ONE IN THE SALOON WHEN I RETURNED belowstairs. My first fear that the men had run off was soon abandoned. The library door was ajar a few inches, and from within I heard Retchling expounding some nonsense that had nothing to do with business. While trying to decide whether or not to enter, I heard a scrabbling sound on the staircase that came up from the kitchen. There in the shadowed area just above the bend stood Jake, beckoning to me. I slipped quietly away from the library before I was seen.

I pulled Jake downstairs a little to avoid detection if Aiglon should decide to return to the saloon. His eager face spoke of great revelations to come.

"What is it, Jake? What did you learn?" I asked.

"He's here, Mick Dougherty!" Jake whispered.

"Where? Is he coming to the front door?"

"Devil a bit of it. He's waiting at the old burnt down."

In local speech, the ruins of Our Lady's Chapel had been shortened to this rustic phrase. Obviously, Mick had arranged to meet his cohorts there, and, equally obviously, either Rachel or myself must go and eavesdrop on their conversation. Most obvious of all was that I would be the one chosen for the job.

"Tell Lady Savage," I ordered. "Slip quietly through the hall, Jake, so they don't hear you. No, better yet, use the servants' stairway. Tell her I've gone to the burnt down and will bring back my report. I'll get there before Aiglon and hide in the bushes."

We both continued down to the kitchen, where Jake turned to the backstairs and I went to the door for my old gray cloak that was kept there in readiness for such rough work as gardening. Meg turned a fiercely demanding eye on me, but I paid her no heed. It was cool in the shadows of evening. Such a tangled garden surrounded Thornbury that every step was menaced by a shadow. A pale gibbous moon rode the sky, but little illumination seeped through to the footpath along which I sped toward the chapel.

When I was still several yards from it, Mickey's mount let out a whinny that frightened me half to death. I moved more stealthily then, creeping forward step by step, peering into the near distance. The humped pile of stones stood out against the dark foliage. When my eyes were totally adjusted to the shadows, I was able to distinguish a dark hump atop the rocks. It was Mickey sitting cross-legged with his head bent down. He was talking to someone, but it couldn't possibly be Aiglon or Retchling, whom I'd left sitting in the library.

The other person was invisible, though the direction in which Mickey was looking told me his companion was concealed by the thornbushes around the chapel. They spoke in low voices, and I crouched down to advance without being seen. My mind was alive with all manner of wild conjecture as to who he was with. Was it no more than an amorous tryst with some local wench? The fact that the other voice was so soft and low suggested it wasn't a man's.

I had to be sure, however, and the only way to get closer without being seen was by skirting behind the bushes. My progress was painfully slow. Every step had to be tried gently for snapping twigs, and during all this while I was missing out on what they were saying. At last I had inched close enough to hear, and even to see dimly through the branches.

It was a woman with him. She wore a shawl over her head and from behind I couldn't tell who she was. Madame Bieler came to mind, but somehow it was impossible to picture her having come to such an inhospitable spot so far out of her way. When Mickey stopped talking, the woman at last spoke, and I very nearly let out a shriek to recognize Rachel's polite accents.

"You don't mean it! Famous, Mickey. You shall be rich, whatever about the rest of us, but did Lord Ware agree?"

"He gave me the commission before he went to London to cart home his statues. And you know I always bend over backward to ingratiate my dear old stepfather, the black-hearted blister."

If this was Rachel's idea of "common civility," one trembles to think how she must entertain close friends! I was so shocked at the manner of their conversation that it took me a few seconds to tune in to its meaning. I couldn't make heads or tails of it. What profitable commission could Lord Ware have entrusted to Mickey Dougherty, and why should he be boasting of it to Rachel in a secret assignation?

"He's not so bad. He's made your mother happy," she pointed out.

"No, Rachel, my pearl, he's only made her a lady. 'Tisn't the same thing, now 'tis it? I'll whisk her back to Ireland with me one of these fine days, if she'll come. But she's promised to love, honor, and repeat every word the old slice says, so likely as not she'll rest where she is. But we're not here to discuss Lady Ware."

"No," Rachel said pensively. "Where could it be?"

Of more interest to myself was *what* it could be they were talking about, and I listened as hard as I could.

"It's not likely it ever was here at all. Sure, the story is as old as the stars," Mickey replied.

"He didn't actually say Our Lady's Chapel, you know," Rachel mentioned.

"Well, what did he say, then?"

"I can't remember it word for word. He mentioned a small stone building standing free from the house—something about the building's being dedicated to his lady's honor or interest, or something of the sort."

"You're a goose, Rachel!" Mickey charged. "*Our* Lady means the Blessed Virgin Mary; *his* lady means Lady Aiglon. He didn't mean the chapel at all. You have to remember Englishmen were all Papists in those days, and better for it, too, if you want an honest Irishman's opinion."

"If I wanted an *honest* Irishman's opinion, I wouldn't ask *you*, Mr. Dougherty. What other small stone building standing close to the house is there? The barn is huge and made of wood. I can't believe the ice house was dedicated to either Lady Aiglon or the Blessed Virgin. It has to mean the chapel."

"Most country ladies get the proceeds from the henhouse. Would it be made of stone at all?"

"Yes, part of it is, but I had it built myself after I came here, so I think we can leave the henhouse out of our consideration," she replied.

"There must have been a belvedere or gazebo or some other stone monstrosity he built for his lady. What you've got to do is look over the old historical documents of the place. I don't plan to spend the rest of my nights digging up the whole demmed estate."

"I'm sure you have much better things to do. Or more amusing, at any rate," she sneered.

"Aye, and more profitable. I'd best go. And, Rachel,

you can tell that ragamuffin lad you've had dogging my steps all day to shab off. I deal fair and square with all my partners.''

"Except for Lord Ware, of course," she inserted, her tone quite toplofty.

"The one and only exception that proves the rule. I'm off to my ladylove now."

"She'll receive you with open arms tonight when you give her back her money." Rachel laughed.

They waved and parted. Mickey threw his leg over his mount and rode off along the path to the main road, and Rachel scuttled out of sight in the other direction. I stood up to let the cricks ease out of my knees before going home. The pale moonlight turned the rocks white and the foliage black, and the setting was so eerie that I almost believed I had dreamed the whole bizarre meeting.

I puzzled over the details of their talk while I walked back to Thornbury. Rachel and Mickey were in league in some scheme to find what they unhelpfully called "it." For Mickey Dougherty to take a shovel in his hands and dig for anything, "it" must be valuable, indeed. Yet its actual existence was apparently based on some ancient story, and its location was lost in the sands of time. The story must have come to light in the old book Rachel had bought in Folkestone. But in that case would she have offered me the book? Not likely! I had to remember how devious Rachel was. She might have offered it on the assumption that I would lose interest after she told me that story about golden chalices and monstrances. And she might also never have intended to let me see the book if I had said yes. She would have conveniently lost it. Well, it was somewhere in her room, and I'd find it and discover what she was up to.

Other branches of the conversation were equally interesting, of course. There was the commission Mickey was performing for Lord Ware, whom he hated. He had some trick up his sleeve there. And most intriguing of all was Rachel's calm statement that Madame Bieler was to get her money back tonight. If Mickey dealt fairly with all his partners, as he had claimed and Rachel had not denied, then Aiglon knew that the money was to be returned. What could possibly have transpired to make Aiglon agree to that after having arranged to have the money stolen himself?

There wasn't a soul in the house I could trust. Willard was in Rachel's pocket with the button closed. Meg didn't care for Rachel, but she was no friend of mine, either, and it was Rachel who paid her salary. As to Aiglon and Retchling, they were worse than the rest. Even Lord Ware, one of my main mental comforts as being approachable at the last moment, had gone off to London to arrange the shipment of his statues.

I slipped in quietly at the back door. Rachel's cloak hung on the peg beside it. Meg looked up from her dish washing and gave me a sulky look.

"Did you tell Lady Savage I was out?" I asked her.

"What would I be telling her anything for?" was her insolent but still satisfying reply. "What's afoot then? Is it my guinea?"

By "my guinea" she meant the bag of gold found in the cellar. Only one of those coins held any interest for her. "No, that's safe, Meg. Finders keepers."

"Hmph," she snorted, but contentedly.

I smoothed my hair before going upstairs. I peeked around the corner to the library. The door was wide open, and the lights were extinguished. The gentlemen would be in the saloon then. If Rachel was with them, I meant to nip upstairs and search her room for the old book. I walked along to the saloon and saw that it was empty. Willard was putting out the lamps.

"Where is everyone?" I demanded.

"The gentlemen have gone out, Miss Pethel. Her ladyship is gone upstairs for the evening."

"Gone out! Where? Does Lady Savage know?"

"I told her myself. She was asking for you, miss."

"Was she, indeed?" I felt the anger gather in my chest and ran up the stairs two at a time to accost her.

I flung open her door without knocking and found her in conversation with Jake, who must have waited all this time to make his report. She gave me an eagle-eyed look and said, "Ah, Constance, there you are. I was looking for you. Jake told me about Mickey being at the old chapel. Did you get there in time to learn anything?"

"Plenty!"

"Good, you can tell me all about it presently. Jake says they've arranged about the boat."

Jake couldn't be satisfied with this poor telling of his adventures. "I followed Mick all the livelong day till my bones are weary. When he went home, I went down to Lord Ware's kitchen to talk to Alfie, my cousin. He carries the wood and coal and slops for his lordship. That's where I learned the whole story. His lordship has got his *Nimble Nymph* up for sale, and her rotting apart at the seams. So Mick, he got a couple of the kitchen lads at it, bailed her out, hammered wood over the holes, and *says* he sold it, but it's hisself that's keeping her for to take them guns to Boney! It's still docked at Lord Ware's place."

I remembered Rachel's coy question as to whether Lord Ware would like the manner in which Mickey executed that vague "commission" and realized that Rachel was in on the whole scheme up to her scrawny neck. She knew what the ship was to be used for. She knew all about that bag of money being passed back and forth. She had managed— how, I would never know—to cut herself in on the profitable and heinous crime of selling arms to the enemy of her own country.

153

I steeled myself to hide what I knew. "Good work, Jake," I said. There was one ally for me, at least. Two—Jake and Jeremy. They were both loyal to the marrow of their bones. They had often spoken of joining the army, but Rachel had talked them out of it.

Rachel smiled and turned to Jake. "Now that we know what boat is chosen and where it is, it won't be necessary for you to do any more following, Jake. You can tell Jeremy the same. Mission accomplished. And don't either of you breathe a word of it, mind!"

"Oh, no, your ladyship. Not a syllabub will leave our lips. Where should I go now?"

"I suggest you go to bed, Jake. You must be dog-tired," Rachel answered.

Jake tugged his lock a few times and backed out the door. Before the door was closed, Rachel turned a glinting eye on me. "And what's your story, Constance?" she asked, attempting a smile that made her face look strangely like a death mask.

"I saw you and Mickey down at the old chapel. I was amazed to see that you had beaten me down. What had Mickey to say?" I looked at her with eager interest, as though I had done no more than look and was mystified still.

After a few seconds of swift calculating as to my veracity and what story she could palm me off with, she spoke. "I happened to spot Mickey's horse from my bedroom window. I saw where he was going and darted down to the chapel to see what he was about. I made sure he'd be meeting Aiglon. Unfortunately, I lost my footing in the dark and he discovered me. I told him I had seen him and feared he was a housebreaker. He knows we're nervous after your scare in the cellar."

"Did he meet Aiglon?" I asked, as though I had swallowed this monumental fib.

"Very likely my being there kept Aiglon away. No, Mickey just made some foolish excuse about wanting to stop and pray. He says the ground there is consecrated or something, and he often stops to commune with God. That should be an interesting communication!"

"Did you know Aiglon and Retchling have gone out?" I asked, curious to see whether this alarmed her.

It didn't. "Yes, but it doesn't matter. They've only gone to the inn for some cards and company. Things are pretty dull here for those city bucks."

I felt some show of concern was necessary from me and said, "Aren't you afraid who they might be meeting at the old chapel. Mickey will be telling them what Jake told us. We know all about it, so we don't have to worry, do we?"

It was impossible not to admire her quick thinking. All the Howells had this incredible ability to lie as easily and convincingly and reasonably as anyone else told the truth. She smiled a very natural-looking smile and said, "I believe I'll just run down to the library and find something light to read. I mean to do my reading in bed."

"I'm going to retire early myself," I answered calmly.

I went to my room, but as soon as she was out her door, I ran back to her room to have a quick look for the Folkestone book. She had locked the door behind her. So she didn't trust me. I wasn't as agile a liar as the Howells. She was following Mickey's advice and looking into old documents to try to discover what small stone building "it" was hidden in or under.

I returned to my own room and closed the door. In a few minutes, Rachel was back. I heard the stealthy twisting of the key in the lock. I sat down and just thought about all the strange, disjointed things that were happening here at Thornbury. Were they all connected in some manner? All were undertaken to gain money illegally, of course, but, other than that, was there any common thread that knitted them into one plot?

It seemed to me that Mickey Dougherty was the common element. He was Madame Bieler's lover and partner in smuggling; he was getting the boat for Aiglon to smuggle the arms to France; he was, right this minute, meeting Madame to give back the money Aiglon had had stolen from her. Aiglon and Retchling weren't meeting Mickey at the inn. God only knew what they were doing, and it was too late to send Jeremy or Jake after them. Would they be meeting with Madame Bieler and Mickey? I wondered. And, on top of the rest, Mickey was involved in some mysterious search with Rachel. Had Rachel used that as a handle to weasel her way into a partnership on the rest of Mickey's misdeeds? She had beat him to the Folkestone book and had that to hold over his head.

And, lastly, what was I to do about any of it? I had no intention of meddling in the smuggling business. Here on the coast it's accepted as practically legitimate employment. Rachel's stealing treasures from Aiglon was nothing new, either, and didn't bother me much. But about selling arms to the French, I could not sit on my chair and do nothing.

The proper and only course was to tell some person in authority what was going on. The constable in Folkestone, Colonel Denby, or Captain Cokewell of the militia. Any one of them would know what to do. I was a little shy about driving alone into the army encampment with hundreds of men and women. If I spoke to the constable, I would have to do it publicly in his office in Folkestone. That could give rise to questions if I were seen. No, Captain Cokewell would serve the purpose. It would not look too odd if I went for a drive on the Leas and stopped off at the church. Or I could go to watch the militia practice. I had never seen them, and they were a popular spectacle.

I felt better now that my decision was made. Time was running out. Tomorrow night was quite possibly the night Aiglon meant to make his move. I could push the worry of Aiglon's and Rachel's treachery from my mind once I had settled with myself what I must do. To completely forget them was another matter. For five years, I had lived with Rachel, and I had become fond of her despite her thieving ways. But she really was a thoroughly dishonest woman. And only see where it landed her. From petty thievery of Aiglon's property, she had graduated to this really serious step. What was the punishment for being a traitor? Hanging?

I closed my eyes, but the head in the noose wasn't Rachel's. It was Aiglon's laughing eyes that mocked me. "You could cure me if you thought it worth your while," he had said. But there was no curing a Howell of lying and deceit. They'd probably cheat Jack Ketch, too, the pair of them.

I don't know how long I sat there, not dreaming exactly, but nightmaring. I was gazing at the window. In the black of night, what was to be seen was a wavy reflection of myself and my room. It was ridiculously early to retire, so I decided to answer Prissy's letter. I reread it first, envying her placid, simple but perfectly happy existence at home. All the hopes of forming not only a suitable but perhaps even a grand attachment that had come with me to Thornbury died that night. It would be a wonderful relief to leave, and I would do so as soon as I had told Cokewell what I must. How could I go on living for one more day among such people as I lived with here?

Halfway through my letter, I tore it up and wrote to Papa instead. I couldn't worry him with the goings-on at Thornbury, but only said that things had changed. Aiglon had come, and soon Rachel would be leaving, so I must come home. I requested that he send the carriage for me as soon as possible. As it was a brief letter, I had time before retiring to begin sorting through my things, deciding what to pack and what to leave behind. I wished I could roll up my memories and toss them in the dustbin as easily as I could my old linens. But I knew they had become permanent residents in my head. There would be no escaping the memories of what had been and the more tantalizing conjectures of what might have been.

CHAPTER THIRTEEN

THE MORNING DAWNED FAIR AND CLEAR. A FEW LAZY puffs of cotton-wool clouds drifted out to sea. It was a fine day for a drive to Folkestone to accomplish my unpleasant duty. No one would question that I wanted to go for a drive on such a day. The only problem would be to get away without company in the carriage. The best hope for that was to leave early, and I made a hasty toilette, hoping to leave before Aiglon and Retchling came down. I wasn't too worried that Rachel would take it into her head to come with me when she had so much research to do on old stone buildings near Thornbury.

I was deeply chagrined to see not only Rachel but also Aiglon and Retchling in the breakfast room when I arrived there.

"Constance, Aiglon has had the most gorgeous notion!" Rachel exclaimed cheerfully. "We are all going to Westleigh for a little holiday."

A holiday at Westleigh was a cherished dream of Rachel's, and one for which she had instilled some curiosity on my own part over the years with her tales of the magnificence to be found there. How was I to refuse without arousing suspicion? I was so busy thinking about an excuse that at first it didn't dawn on me that this was a strange time for Aiglon to be leaving Folkestone. Tonight was the night the guns were to be stolen if my information was correct.

"*All* going?" I asked.

"Yes, and that's only the half of it," she bubbled joyfully. "We are to take a jog up to London first, just you and I. We can be there by evening if we leave soon. Aiglon and Sir Edward will meet us there tomorrow evening. We'll spend another day in London with them and go on to Westleigh in a day or two. What do you think of that, eh?"

I expect that what I thought of that was easily read on my face, for my suspicions soared to learn that Aiglon had no intention of leaving today. No, what he was after was to get Rachel and myself out of the house, leaving him with the perfect freedom to do what he planned to do.

"It sounds lovely, Rachel, but the fact is, I have a ripping headache. I don't feel well enough to tackle a long trip today," I answered.

"You do look a little peaky," she said, staring at my pale face. "Well, it's no matter. We'll put it off till tomorrow. It will give me a chance to pack more carefully and have a few things laundered before I go. Tomorrow will do as well, will it not, Aiglon?"

Aiglon had risen to hold my chair, and I saw the dissatisfaction in his eyes. "A trip in an open carriage might be the very thing to clear up your megrims," he urged.

Rachel answered for me. "Pshaw, it's clear you've never had one in your life, or you wouldn't suggest that a day's travel is the cure for it, my lad. I'll put Constance to bed with a headache powder, and she'll be up in time for dinner. I'll do her packing myself this afternoon, and we'll get an early start tomorrow morning."

Aiglon and Retchling exchanged a questioning glance. What are we to do about them? I read in it. Retchling tried his hand at talking me into quick health.

"London is to me what daffodils are to Wordsworth," he began. "My heart with pleasure fills when I enter a crowded ballroom and see the ladies' feathers dancing like the daffodils by the lake. Lady Moire is having her ball tonight, is she not, Aiglon? Your mama will be going, of course, and will take her visitors with her. Do you have the opportunity to attend many balls, Miss Pethel?"

"No, not many," I admitted, nor did I feel the least urge to attend this one.

Retchling's persuasions had more force with Rachel, and she began to find me looking less peaky. "We could travel with the windows open, Constance, and I could wear my blue shot silk to Lady Moire's ball," she urged.

"Why, you'd be just in time for the great annual sale at the Pantheon Bazaar as well if you went today. It begins tomorrow morning," Retchling outlined. "The greatest bargains are gone by noon. Everyone goes. Lady Aiglon was telling me she got kid gloves for a few pennies last year."

"We both need new gloves, Constance," Rachel reminded me.

"But I really do feel unwell," I insisted, my voice faint.

"That is a pity," Retchling said, shaking his head. "It's the last week for Mrs. Jordan's latest performance at Covent Gardens, too, and Aiglon has a seat on the third tier that will be vacant."

"Oh, no!" Rachel moaned, her heart rent to hear of such wanton waste. "Drink up your coffee, Constance. It's very likely only hunger that ails you. Get her a plate of gammon, Retchling. I'm going to get my headache powder this instant."

Rachel hopped up and left the room, and Retchling filled a heaping platter of food from the sideboard for me. Aiglon poured me a cup of coffee and smiled softly. "It's your last chance, Constance," he said. "By tomorrow, London will have sunk into the Thames, nevermore to be seen. Is your headache really severe, or is it something else that disturbs you?''

I hesitated to meet his gaze. When I did, I saw only a tender concern tinged with a question. I didn't bother trying to answer, for I knew no words would come from my blocked throat.

Retchling set the heaped plate before me. Rachel was soon back with the powder. I took the powder, drank the coffee, and ignored the food.

When Retchling began more temptations, Aiglon shushed him up. ''That's enough nonsense, Beau. We'll all go to London together tomorrow.''

Rachel accepted it. ''I don't know why we ever talked of anything else,'' she said. ''Why was it you gentlemen wished to stay behind for a day?''

''I have a few *pensées* begging to be put on paper,'' Retchling told her. ''These *idées* that come to me are as fickle as a beautiful woman. If I ignore their call, they flee me. What is required is a few hours alone in a quiet scriptorium to wrestle them onto paper.''

''You go ahead and court your *idées*, Retchling. I promise no one will disturb you,'' Rachel replied, unfazed by his high-blown talk. ''Constance will be in bed, and I shall be packing trunks.''

''Trunks?'' Aiglon inquired, his mobile brow rising. ''We're only staying for a few days. Surely one trunk will suffice.''

''I don't suppose Lady Moire is the only lady in London who is giving a ball at the height of the Season! There will be any number of them. Then we shall require country clothes as well for the little sojourn at Westleigh. What is playing at Covent Gardens after Mrs. Jordan closes, Sir Edward? You *do* take your box for the Season, Aiglon?'' Rachel asked.

Some answers were given to these and other questions she fired off to the gentlemen, but I hardly listened. I was figuring how I could get into Folkestone now that I had claimed invalid status for myself. The oft-repeated suggestion that fresh air helped might be useful. I would claim myself well enough for a short drive into Folkestone, but still too weak to tackle a whole day's journey. I'd go to my room for an hour, then try to slip out unobserved.

Aiglon arose to pull out my chair when I said I was going abovestairs. He also accompanied me into the hallway. "You don't seem very eager to taste the sweets of London, Constance. Are you a confirmed country girl?"

"Not at all."

"I see. The reason I ask is that you could skip the London visit and go straight on to Westleigh today if . . ."

I leveled a cold stare that froze the words on his lips. I had never seen him so uncertain. He massaged his chin with his fingers, but his eyes never left mine. "You could cure me if you thought it worth your while," he had said.

I put my hand on his and made one last effort to cure him. "Why don't we all go to Westleigh today?" I asked softly.

For about ten seconds, I thought he was going to do it. I was fool enough to think I was curing him, that he would give up his scheme, turn his back on all the profits, and run off to Westleigh with me. Then he spoke, and the illusion evaporated.

"You know that's impossible, Constance," he said.

I tried to withdraw my hand, but he had placed his other hand over it and held it tightly. "Don't worry. Everything will work out all right. I'm not in any danger."

Such arrogance, such conceit! He thought that it was only his neck I was worried about. That I would accept him whatever he did as long as Westleigh and London were there as bribes.

163

"Aren't you, Aiglon? I wouldn't be too sure about that."

He laughed lightly. "You don't know me very well yet. We haven't had time to plumb the depths of each other's nature. We'll do that at Westleigh quite soon."

"Quite soon," I agreed, and proceeded abovestairs to my room.

I paced and thought and worried until one hour by the clock was up, then slipped quietly belowstairs, got my pelisse and bonnet, and went out through the kitchen to the stables. Aiglon's curricle and grays were gone, and his groom with them. I had Jeremy hitch up the jig and accompany me into town.

Jeremy was unaware of my imaginary headache and chattered as we drove along. "Where are you going to, miss?"

"I believe the militia practices today. I've never seen them. I'm going there."

"Nay, miss. We don't practice in the morning. It's in the evening after chores are done that we meet."

"Are you one of them?" I asked, startled.

"Only since last week. Jake, he's been one forever and shamed me into joining, but I don't get to line up as often as I should because of the distance from town."

"You could borrow a horse or the jig, Jeremy!"

"It's no great matter, miss. I know the procedures, and that's what it's all about. If the stacks were to be blazed, I'd borrow a horse fast enough and go pelting off to join Captain Cokewell. But, like I said, there's no practice in the morning, so where do you want to go instead?"

"To the church."

The Leas had their share of visitors on such a fine spring day. I sent Jeremy off to enjoy the view while I went around to the sacristy to speak to Captain Cokewell. He sat at a desk writing when I entered.

"Ah, good morning," he said, arising to crush my fingers in his large hand. "It's the little lady from Thornbury who was here with Lord Aiglon the other day, isn't it?"

"Yes, Miss Pethel. It is Lord Aiglon I want to speak to you about, Captain."

"Oh, aye. I had a feeling it might have been he that sent you."

"No, no, he didn't send me! He has no idea I'm here."

"Is there more trouble in that quarter?" he asked, moustache twitching.

"Then you knew . . ." That telltale "more trouble" made my revelation easier and confirmed my worst feelings.

"I know all about it, naturally!" he answered, ready to be offended at any slur on his occult powers.

"Oh, thank God! I was half-afraid you wouldn't believe me. Did you know it was Lord Ware's boat that is to be used?"

"Yes, yes," he said, shaking a finger to cut me off and looking all around, lest the walls be listening.

"How did you find out? Who told you?"

"Now, ma'am, it wouldn't do for us to be talking out loud about things that shouldn't even be whispered at such a time. Just rest your worries that we have everything in hand. Not one gun will old Boney get his hands on, and you have my word on it."

Captain Cokewell had a good reputation. His military career had been quite illustrious, and I was reassured to know that he now had full responsibility for what had seemed my own private burden. I was very glad I had come and expressed some such sentiments to him. It set him to twirling his moustache gallantly as he accompanied me to the door. He stepped out into the churchyard with me and inhaled deeply.

"I don't much care for the look of that sky!" he exclaimed, frowning at the beautiful azure-blue arc above us.

"Why, I thought you would like it! Boney will never come on a clear night, folks say. He will sneak in under a blanket of heavy fog and a calm sea."

"But the sea's calm enough," he said with satisfaction.

"Why, Captain, I believe you're looking forward to a chance to meet Bonaparte!" I exclaimed.

He opened his eyes in astonishment, and then laughed. "Well, there's a saying among army men, you know, that old soldiers never die. But this one's getting rusty and wouldn't regret a crack at a worthy enemy."

We parted on the best of terms. I looked across the Leas for Jeremy and saw to my chagrin that he had been accosted by Aiglon. Jeremy didn't know I was supposed to be lying down at home and would certainly have told him I was here. How was I to explain my visit to Cokewell? It would arouse no end of suspicions in Aiglon's mind. Even as I stood, Aiglon glanced up and saw me. He was not in his curricle but advanced on foot. I swallowed nervously and racked my brain for a convincing lie to cover the truth.

Strangely enough, the reason for my visit didn't come up at all. "Constance, you're recovered!" Aiglon exclaimed, smiling from ear to ear.

"The fresh air . . ." I said vaguely.

"Beautiful day, isn't it? What do you say we send Jeremy home and I give you another lesson with the grays? I've got them stabled at the White Hart."

"I didn't tell Rachel I was leaving. She'll be wondering . . ." I answered, for I didn't relish giving him the opportunity for too much close questioning.

"Jeremy can tell her where you are," he parried.

"I don't feel stout enough for a lesson today. Thank you anyway."

"Then I'll drive and you can just sit and rest, lazybones. Come on, I'll throw in a rock for you to sit on to make your drive really pleasant."

"I have so much to do at home. I should be packing . . ."

He took my arm and inclined his head to mine. "Do you have that strange feeling that this has happened before? Last time *you* were determined not to let *me* get away. This time, the shoe is on the other foot. There's no escape. I already told Jeremy to go on home alone. I've got you now, Miss Constance Pethel. There's no evading my vile clutches."

I looked around for the jig and saw its rear wheels departing, with Jeremy in the driver's seat. "So I see. Do you always get your own way, Aiglon?" I asked, deciding to give in with good grace.

"No, I once had a mare with a mind of her own. She wouldn't let me ride her for love or apples or sugar or any other bribe I could think of. And I once had a cousin who was determined to get her toe into Westleigh. I staved her off for ten years, but at last Rachel beat me, too. I think you know what trump card she held. As Mama is not at Westleigh, we required a chaperone. Such hotblooded creatures as Miss Pethel and Aiglon aren't to be trusted alone for a minute."

His manner was playful, and as this line of talk diverted a discussion of my visit with Cokewell, I went along with it. "You've met your match in Rachel. I noticed she even got the red silk out of you."

"She threatens to hang it in the guest room as it's too gaudy for a gown. Or at least too gaudy for a gown for Lady Aiglon. Mama, I mean. But I was the manipulator that time. How was I to see you in the gold without bestowing a piece on Rachel as well, to temper the compliment? More pointed gestures of my intentions must wait awhile."

"What intentions are those, Aiglon?" I asked, but I knew where this intimate talk was headed.

167

"Just what you think, my flower," he answered with the warmest smile ever smiled. Then he tucked my arm under his head and we walked off toward the White Hart.

I couldn't believe Aiglon or any man was capable of being at one time a blackhearted traitor and such a sweet lover. Thoughtful, gentle, generous—yet a consummate liar. He should have been an actor. His forte was convincing people he was what he was not, and I must be wary or he would convince me he was in love with me.

When the curricle was delivered, we drove home at a sedate pace with Aiglon taking the ribbons. I could hardly think of a thing to say, but as Aiglon chattered so easily, my silence wasn't much noticed.

I passed the afternoon in packing my trunk. The trip to Westleigh made an excellent excuse for it, and it had to be done in any case as I planned to go home immediately.

Rachel was in and out of my room a dozen times, ordering me to be sure to pack this and that and telling me what items were not necessary. I nodded and pretended to listen, but what I packed were the gowns I would require at home, not the ball gowns and riding habit she suggested.

"Where are Aiglon and Retchling?" I asked once, and she told me Aiglon had gone out to do a bit of shooting and Retchling was in the library taming his *pensées*. I later looked in the library and saw that it was empty. The men were out arranging their night's work, but I could rest easy. Cokewell would be keeping an eye on them. I could dispense with worry and concentrate on the gnawing regret that sat like a rock in my chest.

The gentlemen sent word via Shiftwell that they would not be dining at home, which finally alerted Rachel to Retchling's absence, but she was not interested in discussing it. I had no idea how deeply she was involved in their

168

affairs, but there was one item that it would look suspicious *not* to discuss with her.

"You realize this is the night the arms are supposed to arrive," I said when we were alone. "That's why Aiglon wanted to get us out of Thornbury."

"I am quite aware of that, Constance," she said matter-of-factly. "They mean to ship them to France on Lord Ware's old *Nimble Nymph.* I had the misery of a cruise on that derelict vessel three years ago, and he hasn't fixed it up since. It scarcely took the weight of the few passengers aboard. There isn't the least vestige of danger that it can carry hundreds of pounds of metal all the way across the Channel. It will sink, hopefully close enough to shore so that the guns can be brought up again. I trust Aiglon will be clever enough to evade capture. He is up to all the rigs, you must know," she added with an air of satisfaction.

This facile explanation was about as reassuring as a shot in the night. "But Mickey did some repairs on the boat," I reminded her.

"Pooh, a few bits of rotting lumber hammered over the larger craters. That scoundrel probably got a fortune from Aiglon for the ship, too." I began to understand her discussion with Mickey at the chapel. *He* would be rich, whatever about the others, she had said, or something to that effect. She had gotten confirmation from Mickey then that the ship was to be used by Aiglon. And I had some assurance from Cokewell that he knew what was afoot, so there was nothing to do but sit on thorns, waiting for Aiglon to be caught in the act of treason.

We went upstairs to finish our packing. I would leave tomorrow by coach. I read the timetable carefully by the light of my lamp, which formed a bright spot of flame on the glass. I marveled that it shone so large and red. For perhaps a full sixty seconds I sat like a moonling, half aware that the candle flame was taking over the whole window glass reflection, before it dawned on me that the light came from outside. Flames leaped into the air, and simultaneously a shrill, piercing scream came bellowing up the stairs.

"Fire! The stacks is ablaze! Boney's landed and we'll all be kilt in our beds." It was Meg, and she was hammering at Rachel's door.

I ran to the window and stared into the night. Certainly the blaze was far enough away to be one of the stacks lit on the coast to alert us of Bonaparte's arrival. It had finally happened, and all I could do was stand with my heart in my throat looking at the window. I was frozen like a stone statue, unable to move a muscle. The murdering, alien horde was probably even now swarming over the beach, pistols cocked, seeking victims. In a flash I saw my body, torn apart and cast aside, while the Frenchies battened themselves at Thornbury. And the only man in the house to rise to our defense was an ancient humpbacked servant who could scarcely walk.

I reckoned without the indomitable Rachel. What was a Bonaparte or a French army to her? Just a new bunch of opponents to get the better of. As I defrosted and sheer, blind panic seized me, Rachel came striding into the room like a general in charge of a regiment.

"Now, then, Constance, we require a little organization here. Meg, shut up, you blubbering idiot! Go to the kitchen and pack up any handy food. Bread, meat, cheese—and have Willard bring the good claret up from the cellar. Put everything in the carriage and have Jeremy harness up the team. In fact, take Aiglon's carriage and team if he hasn't taken them himself."

"Oh, miss!" Meg gasped, fanning her face with her apron tails.

"Run along, Meg. Do exactly as I say. The good claret,

mind. Constance, there's no time to do anything but grab your pearls and sapphire chips and bolt for it.''

"Where can we hide?" I asked, staring, in my stupor, at the bed.

"Hide? Rubbish, there's no point in hiding. They'll batten a troop here at Thornbury, I should think. What we must do is make for Westleigh at all speed. Hurry along, and we'll meet at the carriage. My jewelry box and my money . . ." she muttered, striding from my room. I had a hazy memory of something in her hands. It looked like a book. Yes, the book of Folkestone anecdotes was what she had first picked up to rescue. Even before her jewelry box and her money.

I stuffed my pearls and sapphire necklace in my pocket and looked around the room. The other object I chose to run for my life with was a chipped statue of Venus that rested on my dresser. I never could stand the sight of it, and it was only made of cheap plaster, which gives you some idea of my state. I ran downstairs, leaving my reticule containing four pounds and two shillings on a chair in my room, and carried off a worthless, broken statue.

CHAPTER FOURTEEN

"THAT NO-GOOD JEREMY CHUBB AIN'T IN THE STABLE!" I heard Meg scream as I reached the bottom of the stairs.

"Of course he is. He's sleeping. Rouse him up, Meg, and be quick about it, or we'll all be drawn and quartered," Rachel said impatiently.

"No, he isn't, Rachel. He's joined the militia. He'd have to run to join the regiment at the first sight of the fire," I said.

"Bother. Then you'll have to harness up the carriage yourself, Constance," Rachel said. "I must stay here and make sure everything we need gets packed. You might as well take a load of food out with you."

"But I don't know how to harness up a carriage! I've never done it in my life! Call some of Aiglon's servants."

"They're not here," she announced.

"Where are they?"

"Aiglon gave them the night off. You'll have to do it, Constance. It can't be that difficult. You put the small bits of harness about their heads and leave the reins free for driving."

With these scanty directions, I went trembling in the dark to the stables. There was a feverish something in the very air that night. The horses sensed it and scuffled in their loose boxes, while I tried to figure out which harness was for which horse. Between the trembling of my fingers, the restiveness of the team, plain ignorance on my part, and the poor light, it took me an age to get the team harnessed, and it was all done wrong. Once I had some pieces of metal and leather more or less attached to them and the carriage, I was faced with the job of trying to get the whole contraption out of the stable. While I worked, Meg and Willard came huffing and puffing to put parcels in the carriage. Food and blankets, wine and the box of silver, Rachel's fur-lined cape, Rachel's jewelry box, Rachel's own china, and anything else belonging to her that wasn't too heavy to move.

When it was all packed, there was only room for one in the carriage, and you may be pretty sure who that one was. Between us, we managed to get poor old Willard hoisted into the driver's seat. Meg and myself had to walk until Meg took the notion of climbing up on the postilion's box.

"Constance, take one of Aiglon's mounts. He'll be thankful to you for saving it," Rachel hollered from the coach window.

"They're all gone."

"Bother, the servants must be riding them. And the curricle gone as well, is it?"

"There's only our own horses."

"Well, there you are, hook them up to the jig, and we'll save it as well." On this command, the carriage rattled out of the yard and I was left alone. With the belief that Boney headed toward me even now, I didn't take time to bother with the jig but threw a blanket over the old mare and rode her bareback after the carriage, for I didn't want to lose contact with it.

It was just at the moment we hit the road through the park that the church bells began their dolorous toll, informing the countryside that the awful moment had come. A practice ringing had been done in church one Sunday to teach the parishioners what to listen for. It struck my ear with the force of my own death knell. It obviously had the same effect on Willard, for he whipped the nags to a gallop that soon left me yards behind, hanging on to Dobbin for dear life, while the carriage pulled on ahead of me.

I assumed Rachel would head for Folkestone to meet up with as many people as possible. We hadn't taken the time to light the carriage lights, and by the time I reached the main road, the carriage was long gone, but I turned toward Folkestone and made as much haste as I could. The highway was full of travelers of all degree. Many of them were on foot, some on horseback, some in carts and wagons; all carried more than was convenient, but all they carried was considered essential. One poor woman had a baby at her breast and another by the hand, with the mother and toddler both bawling as loudly as they could.

I shot past them, but my conscience wouldn't let me forget the pathetic sight. I was young, able-bodied, and had no helpless companions. I turned around and went back to the woman.

"Here, you need this more than I do," I said, and held the baby while she clambered aboard, then I handed the baby up to her. There was another Good Samaritan on the road. An elderly man suggested that the horse could take the toddler's weight as well. He would accompany the group to make sure the boy didn't fall off. They set such a laggardly pace that I soon walked on ahead of them. I wasn't actually with anyone, but groups of people were all around, ahead of and behind me. You would have thought they'd be talking, but it was a strangely silent caravan that wended its way to Folkestone. Perhaps they were all listening for the sound of marching soldiers.

I know we all cast our eyes out to sea when the turns in the road allowed us a sight of it. The moon shone silver on the calm waters. A very small stretch of shore was visible to us at any one time, and we had at least the reassurance of seeing that no French flat-bottomed boats were harbored directly below us. Every twist and bend of the road brought a new fear that they would come into sight. Our steps would speed up as we approached these corners, then slow down when we saw the empty shingle beach where the wet pebbles gleamed in the cold moonlight.

It was hard to walk in slippers designed for the saloon. I felt every stone and bump through the thin leather soles, and from time to time pebbles found their way inside my slippers to slow me down as well. After a few miles of travel, I had to stop to remove the stones from my slippers and to rest my legs. I went off to the side of the road and sat on a milestone. A blister had formed on my left heel, and I tried wadding my handkerchief up to use as protection. Strange how such a trivial exigency could exert itself above the much deeper terror of the invasion.

I drew a deep sigh and looked up at the hilltops to see that a series of stack were ablaze now. The first fierce flames of the furze had long since burned out, and it was the more sluggish turf that burned on. The moving figures of the men at the fires looked like black shadows. They didn't even have guns with which to defend themselves and the helpless citizens. I remembered that this was the night the guns were to have been delivered and felt a moment's satisfaction that Aiglon's plans had gone awry. But it was a short-lived satisfaction. He wouldn't be shipping the guns to France because the French were here, around one of the dark bends in the road, waiting to pounce.

When I looked at the road, I realized that the crowd had passed me by. They were getting away from me, and I was on thorns to attach myself to whatever safety their numbers conferred. I tied my slipper and braced myself to rejoin the caravan. I took one step, then stopped. What was that noise? A tangle of bush grew at the side of the road, and from within its invisible depths issued a rustle. A Frenchie! They had spread out from their landing spot and were creeping about the countryside to murder us one by one. I froze, praying that he hadn't seen me. There was another rustle, and I took to my heels. Not down the road—I'd have to run right past him to do that. No, I ran back, and when there was a break in the bush, I scampered up the hill toward the closest rick. At least there would be one or two Englishmen there to help protect me.

I looked over my shoulder once as I ran, but saw nothing. I didn't tempt fate by stopping or by returning to the road. I scrambled up that hill like a mountain goat, digging into the earth with my fingers to keep my footing, for it was very steep. A sharp pain grew in my chest, but I forged on, clinging to roots and bushes and outcrops of rocks till I crested the hill.

When I reached the top, I realized that I had run to the largest rick. It was just outside of Folkestone, and it was the one that was to be lit to pass the signal down the coast. The Leas and the Church of St. Mary and St. Eanswith were just a few hundred yards beyond it. The militia would be gathered there, and I was as safe as anyone could be at such a time.

At any rate, I could see that the man stoking the fire was an English farmer in fustian and a battered cap. I didn't stop but ran on, my feet dragging now, to the church. There stood Captain Cokewell with his ragtag and bobtail troop of militiamen formed into a marching group, armed with pikes and shovels and any old stick they could grab hold of. The townspeople hovered in a frightened half circle around their defenders. I asked the woman beside me what the militia was going to do, and she told me they had sent out runners and were waiting to hear in which direction they should march.

"Two of the runners have come back already, and it's beginning to seem that it was all a false alarm," she told me hopefully.

"How could such a thing happen?" I asked, yet I, too, felt a surge of hope that she was right.

"There's whispering it was done as a prank by some young lads. They ought to be whipped if that's what it is," she said sternly.

"It's hard to believe anyone would do such a thing!"

"It was none of our local boys, and that's for certain," she told me, emphasizing this with a nod of her head. "But there's been a new young bunch of fellows from London hanging about the town lately. I expect that's their idea of a romp, to go scaring the daylights out of honest women and children. That's some fine example his lordship is setting, is all I have to say!"

"His lordship?" I asked, but I already had a good idea of what she'd reply.

"Aye, young Aiglon and his crew. I knew they were up to no good hanging about with Dougherty and that French madame of his. That's who's behind this fracas, see if it isn't. And never a step will be taken to chastise them, either," she added angrily.

My own first reaction was of rightful indignation like the woman I was talking to. It took a minute or more before the other possibility occurred to me. Aiglon had had the fires lit, all right, but it wasn't just a harmless prank. He had done it for a purpose. It was a distraction to keep the militia busy while he absconded with the guns!

I flew forward and grabbed Captain Cokewell's arm before timidity could prevent me, for it was hard to run out into the field in front of the assembled group and make a spectacle of myself.

"Not now, Miss Pethel," the captain said, shaking off my arm.

"This is urgent. Desperately important! Don't you see? Aiglon has done this to tie you up while he seizes the shipment of arms!" I told him.

"Good gracious, what put that in your head?" he asked, looking at me as though I were a moonling.

"This is the night they arrive!"

"No, no, *tomorrow* night, Miss Pethel."

"I tell you it's a trick! You've got to stop him."

"My job is to stop Napoleon Bonaparte, miss, and I'd be grateful if you'd let me do it!" he hollered. He shook me off into the shadows in disgrace.

He didn't believe me. And neither would anyone else. I was the only person in the whole town who knew what was happening at Lord Ware's dock just a scant few miles away. There was a little bay there, which made that bit of the coast invisible from town. But what could I do? I didn't even have a gun. And I didn't have transportation, either.

That last necessity wasn't impossible to overcome. There were any number of carriages and mounts gathered around the Leas. I edged to the back of the throng, aware of the curious eyes following me, but soon the crowd's attention was diverted by the show Cokewell and his men were putting on. I stood quietly until no own was looking, and during this time I picked out my mount. There was a white mare tethered to a tree a little apart from the others. Best of all, there was a pistol wrapped in fustian and attached to the saddle. Several of the wagons had hunting guns in them, too, but a horse would be easier to get away on.

I eased myself toward the white mare, unfastened her line, and walked her off a few yards from the throng. No one seemed to notice. As soon as I got behind some trees, I pulled myself up into the saddle and took off. I wished I had Jeremy and Jake or some men with me, but there was no one I recognized or trusted. They were somewhere in that troop of Cokewell's, impossible to get at. The mare didn't like having an unknown rider and gave me some trouble at first, but I spoke gently to her until I was beyond hearing, then urged her on to a gallop.

When I reached the highway it was deserted. There wasn't a soul on the road except me. I had the eerie sensation of being the last person alive in the world. I flew through the black night, with the white moon shining down on me, hastening to Lord Ware's home. I recognized the perimeters of his land when I reached his spinney and took the short cut through it. Here the moonlight vanished, and I picked my way more slowly along the horse trail, listening for any unusual sounds.

Ware Castle soon rose up in the distance, a great, gray, stone giant brooding over the water. I saw lights in two of the upper windows before I could see the bottom part of the house. When I was close enough that I required more stealth, I dismounted and went forward on foot, not forgetting to unwrap the pistol and take it with me. There was a bare, unprotected area between the spinney and the house, which I traversed by hunching down low and running as fast as I could.

Soon I was in the home garden, with the rear wall of the castle before me. I wanted to go around to the front, which would give me a view of the sea and what was going forth there. I flattened myself against the wall, thankful for my gray gown which disappeared against the stone facade. I inched forward, ears cocked. Before I reached the front of the building, I heard stealthy sounds. There were a few words spoken in voices I didn't recognize. I didn't recognize the words, either, for they were in colloquial French. Any doubt that I had been mistaken in my fears now vanished. This was the time and the place where the guns were being sold to the French. There was only one more point to verify, and that was that Aiglon was a part of it.

I crept forward, inch by inch, till I could peek around

the front of the castle. There was a whole line of huge crates there, and in the darkness of night, men were unloading heavy boxes and carrying them down to the wharf, with two men for each box. One box had its top removed, revealing guns packed in sawdust. At the wharf, Lord Ware's old ship had a gangplank placed to allow easy loading of the cargo. I tried to count the number of men and lost track at eighteen. How was I ever to stop so many armed men? For they *were* armed. In fact, it was the duty of two husky brutes to do nothing but stand with pistols cocked, looking all around for intruders.

I recognized Mickey Dougherty. He stood just at the top of the gangplank directing the loaders where to stow the boxes. I looked around for Aiglon, praying he wouldn't be there. There was the sound of a door opening, and suddenly two of the Frenchies turned toward the castle. *"C'est le patron,"* one of them said. I waited to see who would emerge as the chief of the operation. Would it—impossible thought—be Napoleon Bonaparte himself? The boots that strode down the steps had an arrogant, imperial sound to them. My heart beat like a drum in my throat during those interminable few seconds while I waited for *le patron* to show himself.

He strode boldly out into the white moonlight, and I recognized the unmistakable outline of Lord Aiglon. He rattled off some French. One of the French guards darted away and returned with their leader. The man in charge of the French part of the expedition carried something in his hand, some sort of bag. He delved into it with his other hand, and come out with a fistful of golden coins. They poured from his fingers like rain to be caught in Aiglon's outspread hands. Fury burned in my throat. And still I had not come up with a reasonable means of stopping this despicable treachery.

Lights were called for. Aiglon examined the coins, hefted

them, rubbed his fingers over their surface to be sure he wasn't receiving counterfeit. At last he appeared to be satisfied and called for *"le vin pour tout le monde."* Right there, in front of Lord Ware's castle, wineglasses were distributed and wine poured.

Mickey Dougherty wasn't likely to pass up a glass of wine and came running to join the party. "Let's not dally with this, Aiglon. Get them shoved away from shore *aussitôt que possible*, and all that," Mickey advised.

"You underestimate me, Mick. The burning stacks will keep the town and Cokewell entertained for several hours. Best to leave nothing to chance," Aiglon replied, as calmly as though he were in a polite saloon. He even proposed a toast in French.

And still I didn't see my way clear to tackling so many men. I thought if I could get either Aiglon or the French leader at my gun's point, the others might do as they were told, but I was by no means sure of it. The cowardly thought occurred that I could always have the English half of this team arrested after the French had escaped and at least bring them to justice. But then those crucial guns, which were needed here, would be off to France to arm Boney's waiting soldiers. No, I had to do something now before the arms left in that boat.

It was either desperation or lunacy or both that propelled me from the shadows. No one noticed me as I glided forth. I advanced a few steps and drew a target on Lord Aiglon's chest. And then I didn't know what to say. The most frightening words I knew were those spoken by highwaymen, so I said, "Stand and deliver." My voice shook, but my gun held fairly steady.

A shocked silence settled over the men. They looked at each other, then to their respective leaders for orders. It was Mickey who recognized me.

He uttered some unrepeatable curses, ending in the words, "By God, it's Constance Pethel!"

Aiglon didn't say a word. He peered through the shadows, trying to determine whether it was indeed me. The moon shone full on his face, turning it a ghastly white. He looked like a statue dressed up in a topcoat and breeches. I was so busy staring at him that I missed what the others were doing. I didn't realize that part of the tableau had come to life, that the French *patron* had drawn his pistol and cocked it. I just saw Aiglon's arm fly out, and later thought that he was trying to deflect the bullet's direction. I saw a flash of orange from the Frenchman's gun, heard a deafening roar, and jumped back. My head hit the corner of the stone castle, and I was momentarily stunned by the impact.

When I opened my eyes, I was lying flat on the ground, being examined for bullet wounds by Aiglon, who was cursing a blue streak. I sat up and saw that Mickey was harrying the Frenchies aboard. I had failed. My head reeled with the shock of sitting up. Blue and purple wheels spun in crazy circles, bright yellow spears flashed in between, and somewhere in the dim background was the creak of sails being raised and their direction taken. As it was too late to do more, and as I had failed so miserably, dying seemed like a good idea. I closed my eyes and tried to die, but my ears went on tending to business. They recognized the sound of Mickey's voice.

"There's a good night's work then," he said cheerfully. "What seems to ail Constance?"

"I don't feel any blood," Aiglon replied. His hands traveled up my neck, over my head, and back down my body. I pushed them away weakly, but they continued to flutter over me.

"She's keeled over with shock at such a mauling as

you're giving her. Constance isn't used to that kind of carrying on. How'd she know we were here?'' Mickey asked.

''How the hell should I know?'' Aiglon growled, and raised my head onto his arm. ''Constance. Constance, speak to me,'' he ordered. His voice was ragged with worry.

''Traitor!'' I tried to sneer it, but it came out in a whining, mewling whimper. His face was a blurred, black scowl above me.

''I see you'll have your hands full talking away this night's work,'' Mickey said. ''I'll go and bring Cokewell and a few of the lads to help us round up our French friends. It shouldn't be too long. I wish I could stick around for the show.''

''Go ahead,'' Aiglon said distractedly. When he spoke again a moment later, his voice was much firmer. ''Drop the bag, Mick.''

''Now if I didn't go and forget I'd picked it up at all.'' Mickey laughed and tossed the bag of gold at Aiglon's feet.

I feared my brains had become addled by my fall. Why would Mickey bring Cokewell when they had succeeded so well in evading him all night? Their French friends had already left. The show was over except for the show of concern Aiglon was putting on for my benefit. He was trying to pull my head against his chest while he comforted me with soothing phrases.

''Get your hands off me, you despicable wretch!'' I said, wrenching away from him.

He released me at once and threw his hands up in the air as though still at gunpoint. ''That ain't no way to treat a hero, Constance,'' he cautioned.

''You may be a hero to your French pals; don't expect any medals from King George!''

"My darling idiot, you've already made a jackass of yourself tonight. Don't make yourself a flaming jackass."

His words were hard, but his smile was soft. Though I hadn't yet figured out what was going on, I knew it wasn't what I had thought and feared. "Oh, Aiglon, have I really?"

"Most assuredly, a prime jackass."

"I'm so glad!" I breathed, and went into a real, honest-to-goodness swoon in his arms.

My head ached abominably. My blistered heel was burning; every muscle in my arms and legs ached from my long walk, the climb up the hill, and the exertion of riding astride when I wasn't accustomed to it. I hadn't put on a pelisse when I fled the house, and it was freezing cold by the water. I didn't even want to think of how I must look, but, in spite of it all, I was at peace.

Then I realized that Aiglon was restless. Once he was convinced I wasn't seriously hurt, he began moving his position about to get a look at the sea. "What are you doing, Aiglon?" I complained.

"I'm just looking at the boat," he answered vaguely.

"The navy is going to intercept it, isn't it?" I asked. "The French aren't going to get away with our guns at all."

"No, the navy has nothing to do with this."

"But how are you going to get the guns back?"

"What guns? There aren't any guns on that boat."

"I saw them with my own eyes," I insisted. It occurred to me that I might not have gotten to the bottom of the story yet, but I was loathe to make a greater fool of myself than I already had.

"Sometimes things aren't what they seem, Constance."

He stood up and peered out to sea. I got to my feet and did the same. "I'm very glad to hear it," I said, "for it certainly seems to me that you sold those guns to the Frenchies, and the boat is rapidly sailing to France.''

"Yes, it looks that way, doesn't it?'' he asked. There was a frown pleating his brow.

"If you counted on Mickey Dougherty to perform any vital part of this plan, Aiglon, you're a worse jackass than I am.''

"Oh, my God! You don't suppose he double-crossed me?'' Aiglon gasped.

"A flaming jackass,'' I said weakly.

CHAPTER FIFTEEN

"AIGLON, THAT BOAT IS SINKING!" I EXCLAIMED. IT TOOK me two or three minutes to realize it, for its submersion into the sea was slow. As it pulled straight away from shore, nothing unusual could be detected, but as it tacked out of the bay into the channel, it was perfectly clear that the stern was listing badly. "The guns are going to be lost! Do something, Aiglon! Cokewell needs those guns desperately!"

He looked down at me and smiled a reckless smile that belonged on a buccaneer's swarthy face. "Yes, I really must leave you now, my Inconstant one. Duty calls."

He was gone, and after he'd taken a dozen paces, he was lost in the shadows of the night. I didn't know what he was doing until I saw a sleek prow pull out into the bay following the Frenchmen's boat. I darted down to the wharf, and though visibility was imperfect, I was pretty sure it was Retchling at the helm. Various dark forms darted about, one of them presumably Aiglon. I didn't recognize the ship, but I knew it wasn't Mickey's lugger. It skimmed speedily, effortlessly through the water like a shark or a mermaid. As soon as the simile occurred to me, I tentatively identified the ship.

The next few minutes were very interesting, indeed. I

envisaged a chase, a minor sea battle, but it was nothing of the sort. The *Mermaid* could easily have overtaken the other boat, but she trimmed her sails and dallied about till the other boat sank slowly into the sea, its cargo lost forever. I understood then that her function was to pick up the French sailors who had plunged into the water to avoid going down with their ship. By the eerie silver light of the moon, I saw the French being hauled aboard. As no mutiny ensued, I assumed that one of Aiglon's men was cajoling them into docility with a gun. It was a well-managed affair but for the little matter of having lost our guns!

It occurred to me, as the *Mermaid* returned to shore, that keeping a savage bunch of Frenchmen in line would be less than peaceful, and was very relieved when Cokewell, Dougherty, and about half of the militia arrived at Ware Castle. They ran down to the dock and stood, a fearsome sight, with their axes and shovels, and, in a few cases, their guns, at the ready. Personally, I'd prefer death by bullet to death by an axe. I began to think those rude arms had been underestimated. The blades glinting in the moonlight lent a barbaric touch that would frighten any enemy to death.

I had the glory of being the only female in all of Folkestone and its environs to witness the capture of the French bandits. To avoid being a nuisance to the men, I hung quietly in the background to learn what I could. As soon as Aiglon had leaped to shore, he went running toward Captain Cokewell, and I eased closer to listen.

"I'm not entirely happy with this affair, Lord Aiglon," Cokewell said. "My understanding was that it was to be *tomorrow* night." The rough timbre of his voice suggested that his moustache would be jiggling.

"Unfortunately, things speeded up at the last minute and we had to move swiftly. With the invasion alarm throwing us all into confusion, it was impossible to ask you to join us. I knew you had more important things to do. The safety of the people is in your hands,'' Aiglon explained, with a few more splatters from the butter boat to ease Cokewell's ire.

"That's true. I couldn't have abandoned my post, but I regret missing this little skirmish all the same,'' he answered, somewhat mollified. "But the arms are safe, are they?''

I perked up my ears to hear how Aiglon would explain away this contretemps. "Safe as a babe in his mother's arms. They're in Lord Ware's cellar.''

"What the devil are they doing there? They were to be dropped off at my depot!'' Cokewell howled.

"True, but the last time they were headed to your depot, they went astray, as you may recall,'' Aiglon reminded him. "It's been decided in London that each volunteer will take his rifle to his own home. In that way, no mass theft is possible, and the men will have their guns near them at all times.''

"Trust London to come up with some impracticable plan,'' Cokewell complained, but he was so eager to see the arms that he soon pressed on to demand a trip to Lord Ware's cellar.

Apparently what he saw there pleased him. He was in his element during the next half hour setting guards on the Frenchies, marching them off to Folkestone, and arranging temporary safety for the arms in the cellar and eventual transportation of them to town.

If one person enjoyed the night more than Cokewell, it was Retchling. A new side of him surfaced. I daresay his managing powers were even more muscular than his *Pensées*. He prodded a gun into the prisoners' backs with great relish and threatened the most dire consequences if they so much as looked a revolt.

188

Mickey Dougherty was hanging around the edges of the group, keeping a surprisingly low profile. When I could learn nothing from Aiglon about how the guns had magically not been on the ship when I saw them being loaded with my own eyes, I decided to ask Mickey.

"One box of guns had to be sacrificed," he admitted sadly. "We knew the Frenchies would want one opened."

"But how did you know which one they would open, and what was in the others?" I asked.

"That's where my particular familiarity with the French breed was helpful to his lordship." He smiled modestly. "I was able to tell him they'd demand that the box on the very bottom of the pile was the one to be hauled out and opened, so that's the one we had guns in. We loaded the others up with rocks. Packed in sawdust to muffle the sound, you know. The shipment arrived here this afternoon. You'd have heard maybe that my stepda bought a great load of stone statues for his garden? They came all crated, by sea, and were put ashore this very afternoon." A broad wink explained what was really in the crates.

"Will his lordship mind that you used the castle for this job, Mickey?" I asked. Ware was known to be temperamental where his stepson was concerned. More temper than mental, actually.

"He was in alt. Especially to see I was on the side of the angels—for a change," Mickey admitted bluntly. "He wanted to be here for the show himself, but my mama was helpful in getting rid of him. They're dancing their dear hearts out this minute at Lady Moire's ball in London."

I ransacked my mind for any other details that had been nagging and asked, "Did Aiglon set the bonfires on purpose tonight?"

"Devil a bit of it. He was here all along. Firing the

stacks was Shiftwell's contribution to the project. We had to keep old Captain Moustache busy, or he'd have had a regiment here to alert the Frenchies that something was afoot. At first, Aiglon took the cork-brained notion that Cokewell might have been the loose screw in losing the first batch of arms, you know. He was one of a small handful that knew when and by what route they were coming. We kept him half in the dark all along, though Aiglon *did* give him *some* explanations. Enough to keep him quiet," Mickey explained.

"How did you ever convince Aiglon to trust you, Mickey?" I asked. "I imagine you were one of that small handful as well."

"I was, and no denying it. But then I've embraced the old Blarney stone as often as I've embraced a lady, so I have a little ease of talking my way out of a corner, as you might say. Now don't look at me like that, my flower. It was all a misunderstanding about . . ."

He gave me a wary look. The blank incomprehension on my face told him I was less aware of things than he had assumed, and he fell silent. "What was a misunderstanding? Who *did* sell the information to the French the first time? I hope they catch the traitor and hang him," I said vehemently.

"Ah, there was no treason in it at all. 'Twas a misguided act of patriotism is all it was. You English are a blood-thirsty lot, and unforgiving." He shook his head sadly and walked away.

It was another hour before the French prisoners had been hauled away and before Cokewell and the militia had either left or were doing guard duty on the guns.

"It's time we all go into the saloon and celebrate with a bottle of my stepda's finest," Mickey declared.

Aiglon, Mickey, Retchling, Aiglon's servants, and I went into Lord Ware's saloon and were treated to a few bottles of champagne. There was a loud, self-congratulatory discussion of the night's activities. At one point, Aiglon and Mickey drifted off to the far side of the room for some private conversation. It wasn't entirely peaceful, to judge by the gesturing of hands and the scowling expressions, but eventually they came to terms and rejoined us.

I happened to glance at the long-case clock in the corner and noticed that it was three o'clock in the morning. "Good gracious, look at the time! I've got to get home! Rachel will be wondering what happened to me!" I exclaimed.

"How did you get here, Constance?" Retchling asked. The formality of "Miss Pethel" had been abandoned with the second glass of champagne.

"I stole a horse and gun," I said, yawning, and looked around for the gun.

Mickey picked it up and examined it. "It'd be John Forman's old white mare you borrowed. At least this is his weapon. It would have blown up in your face if you'd tried to fire it. Just tell me where you tethered the nag, Constance, and I'll see it's returned."

"I'll have to drive it to Thornbury. I can't walk home!"

"Every man in the room except myself is going to Thornbury. One of them can squeeze you into his rig," Mickey said, shaking his head at my foolishness. It was fatigue that rendered me so obtuse.

When we all prepared to leave, it turned out that Aiglon's servants had ridden and Retchling had come to Ware Castle in the curricle with Aiglon. Retchling borrowed the stolen mare, leaving me to occupy the other seat in the curricle. I wished it had been the closed carriage, for I just wanted to curl up and fall asleep. The night air was chilly, but Aiglon had a rug in which I swaddled myself for the trip. A few details still bothered me, and before my eyelids closed, I asked Aiglon about them.

"Did you find out who it was that's responsible for losing that first shipment of arms?" I asked.

"Madame Bieler weaseled their route and time of arrival out of Mickey. He's convinced me he had no idea she meant to steal the guns. She was wise enough not to try to enlist his help. It seems she has wide-flung connections with the French element in England. She sells silks to ladies as far away as Wight and even London. At times, there are messages wrapped up in the parcel, I expect. It makes a simple means of communication. All of her messages weren't *billets-doux*, as mine was."

"I wouldn't put it past Mickey to have been in on it himself." I yawned, ignoring his taunt.

"No, I acquit him of that. When he learned of it his anger was genuine. It was a share of the money he first lamented, you see. That had a touch of unrehearsed honesty to it that convinced me," Aiglon said, smiling. "I agreed to help him relieve Madame of her ill-gotten gains. He knew where she stashed her gold, in the cellar of her shop, but in the end we had to give it back, or she couldn't have bought this second load—of rocks. Catching Madame and her crew was the main thing, but we got the money in the end, too, so it's no matter."

"Mickey didn't get it, though," I pointed out. "The money, I mean."

"No, but he got his stepda's approval, which is an entirely new thing for him. Ware could do something fine for Mick if he would bestir himself. I, for one, would like to see him suitably settled."

"Don't count on it."

"He has a flexible conscience, to be sure. I must count this bag of gold when we get home. But he's as willing to forgive others as himself. He feels no rancor toward Madame. She's French, and for her to help her own people is seen as patriotism, not treachery. I'm afraid I have to agree with him there," Aiglon said. "I'd do much the same thing if I were living in France. But I'm not, so Madame had to be apprehended."

"Did you think to have someone keep an eye on Madame during these proceedings?" I asked. The cold night air was reviving me. Or perhaps I had passed beyond sleep.

"It was the job of the constable at Folkestone to lock her up at the signal of the bonfires. We had to let him in on that trick, but it seems he didn't give us away."

"You put the whole countryside through a deal of unnecessary bother, Aiglon."

"No, actually I was astonished Cokewell had never had a dress rehearsal," he objected. "There ought to have been one to prepare the citizens for the real thing. One hopes it won't happen, of course, but it's best to be prepared."

"It certainly caught Rachel and I off guard," I admitted. "But she was marvelous! You'll be happy to hear she saved your carriage and team."

"For that I can forgive her much," he said. "Who's driving them?"

"Willard. I harnessed them up for him . . . sort of."

At this speech, Aiglon whipped his grays to a faster pace, muttering fears and threats as to the safety of his animals. It became clear at the first corner that his passenger was in more danger, for I nearly fell out of the curricle. My arms were hobbled by the blanket, and this prevented me from holding on as tightly as I should have. He slowed the team to a trot then and put his arm around me for greater safety and better lovemaking.

"So far I've been doing all the explaining, old flower," he said, inclining his head to mine and lowering his tone

193

to flirtation. "Now let's hear the tale of the stolen horse and useless pistol. Just what brought you to Ware Castle? Most of all I'm curious to learn why you aimed the thing at my poor self and not the Frenchie!"

"I'm too tired to do the story justice," I objected, resting my head on his chest.

"Try. I thought I had convinced you I was on the right side. Though, to be sure, I *did* have a doubt when your headache came on so suddenly this morning. When it recovered in time to send you off to Cokewell, my doubt soared toward certainty. Your expression, a gentle blend of guilt and regret, assured me Cokewell hadn't revealed what he knew of my plans."

"I guess it was the night you and Retchling met Mickey at the old burnt-down that I started wondering."

"The old burnt-down what?" he asked in confusion.

"The chapel, of course."

"Of course! It is the fact of its not having burned down that confused me. It was knocked down by Cromwell's firebrands, according to the manuscripts at Westleigh."

"Anyway, Rachel sent me to listen at the kitchen door that night while you talked over your plans," I said sleepily. "Beau said the F.O. wouldn't like what you were doing, so I believed it was something illegal."

"Oh, they like *what* I'm doing right enough, they just wouldn't care to know beforehand exactly *how* I meant to do it, as a few laws had to be twisted. For one thing, they didn't share my suspicion that someone in the militia was leaking information about strategic shipments. But I knew none of my people in London were responsible. That left Cokewell and whoever he had told of it here. I expect my paying a little too much of the government's money for Lord Ware's derelict boat won't go down too well, either. Fortunately, they didn't know the state of its hull and how

194

easy it was to arrange for it to sink. That was part of the bribe to ensure Mickey's help,'' he explained. ''It was a good investment in the long run.''

''*Part* of the bribe? Yes, I remember you saying you had an ace up your sleeve. You haven't paid Mickey for the boat yet, and he's taking a good part of the money to keep for himself. Is that it?''

''I don't know what larceny he may have in mind there, but, as I said, that's part of it,'' Aiglon answered.

''What's the other part?''

''You're too guileless, Constance. I anticipate a good measure of fun with Rachel over the other part, and if you knew, that creature would have it out of you in seconds.''

''She's worked her way into Mickey's confidence. I know that much,'' I murmured.

''And vice versa.''

''I know she knew all about using Ware's boat and why he gave Madame back the money and all that. What excuse was Madame given to account for recovering it?''

''I believe Mick fabricated some story about one of his smugglers having stolen it. I stopped by her shop with you the next day to try to gauge her attitude toward me. It was crucial to know whether she had connected me with any of the unusual goings-on.''

''She didn't appear to. I think she connected you with a possible new source of income entirely.''

''That's why I was at pains to let her believe my pockets were to let,'' he said. His voice seemed to be coming from far away. ''Only for Mick's sake, of course,'' he added to annoy me.

I was warm and comfortable wrapped up in the blanket and Aiglon's arms. The regular *clip-clop* of the grays was as peaceful as a lullaby. I dozed off to sleep about halfway between Folkestone and Thornbury, and when I opened my eyes again, I was being lifted bodily from the curricle by Aiglon. We were home. The windows of Thornbury were all aglow, which told me that Rachel and Willard and Meg had gotten here before us. How happy I was to be back! When I had left several hours ago, I feared I would never see Thornbury again.

"It's so good to be home," I said.

"In my arms, you mean?" Aiglon asked, and began walking toward the door.

"No, I just meant back at Thornbury. You'd best put me down, Aiglon. Rachel would be scandalized to see me being carried."

"She'll have to get used to it," he objected, but he did set me on my feet.

We walked together to the front door with his arm around my waist. "Do you suppose Rachel would be scandalized to see me kiss you good night, too?" he asked with his hand on the knob.

"Outraged, sir. And so would I."

"Then you must close your eyes, Constance," he warned, and swept me into his arms for a good-night kiss that sent my senses reeling. I thought that night had brought more than enough new experiences, but this kiss was more surprising than all the rest. It was tender and fierce, frightening and reassuring; it was demanding and giving, a promise and a fulfillment; it was too long and much too brief. In short, a perfectly satisfying kiss. Most surprising of all was that Aiglon was able to speak as soon as he released me, while I was quite certain my lungs had collapsed or burst.

"You can open your eyes now," he said.

"Oh, I thought I had fallen asleep," I gasped, embarrassed to be caught in such a ridiculous position, standing up straight with my eyes closed.

"I've quite overwhelmed you with my ardor, I see. I

196

don't usually put them to sleep on their feet. Go to bed, Constance. I'll do better tomorrow, and that's a promise.''

Then he opened the door and we went in.

CHAPTER SIXTEEN

YOU MAY JUDGE FOR YOURSELF HOW THE INVASION SCARE
rocked the very foundations of everyday life when you hear
what greeted our eyes upon entering the saloon. Of Rachel
there was no sign, but comfortably ensconced on the best
gold-plush sofa were Willard and Meg, with a bottle of
brandy, a jug of water, and two glasses on the table between them. Before Aiglon or I had a chance to speak,
Meg squinted her eyes at me and said, "She knows we're
here," in a most testy voice.

Poor old Willard tried to get to his feet, but age or perhaps brandy got the better of him, and he only rose up
halfway.

"We're very relieved to see you got safely home," Aiglon said. "Do you happen to know if my servants have
arrived yet, Willard?"

Willard's head had settled on Meg's shoulder. He half
opened his eyes, smiled inanely, and snorted. "Slap-bang
team. First-rate fiddler . . . bloods . . . drove 'em . . ."

These were oblique references to his having driven Aiglon's team. Meg was quick to remove the worried frown
from Aiglon's brow. "Your horses are safe and sound in
the stable, never fear, and your servants in my kitchen."

"Where is Lady Savage, Meg?" I asked.

"Gone to bed hours ago," Meg replied, and began gathering up the empty glasses.

"You should do the same," Aiglon advised me.

"So should you."

"Yes, and so I shall, as soon as I check my bloods. *A demain.*" He executed a small bow and fled to the stable.

I stood at the bottom of the stairs, looking up and wondering if I could make it or if I should go back to the saloon and sleep on a chair. Finally, I dragged my tired body and sore feet up by clinging to the bannister for support.

In my room, I lit the lamp and glanced in the mirror at a strange and extremely disheveled lady. Her hair was blown around her face in wild abandon. As for her face, it was streaked with dirt and dust, and the gown was the same. A large rent left her skirt hanging open for twelve inches, displaying the plain cotton petticoat beneath.

I lifted a hand to tidy my hair and saw the dirt beneath my nails from scrabbling up the hill to the bonfire. Two nails were broken to the quick, and one knuckle was skinned. I looked for the world like a street urchin who hadn't washed for a month. To top off this calamitous spectacle, I was smiling like a moonling. I wondered how Aiglon had had the stomach to take me into his curricle, let alone his arms.

It would require at least an hour to clean myself, and then I would have to do it with cold water, so in the end I merely removed my gown and went to bed in my petticoat and filth. I slept like a baby, too. By morning I was refreshed enough to tackle the monumental job of making myself presentable. Before I set toe downstairs, I bathed and changed, coerced my hair into some semblance of order, filed the rough edges of my fingernails, and put a plaster on my heel. I felt nearly human again, and was extremely curious to hear the details of Rachel's night.

She was at the breakfast table with Aiglon and Retchling when I went down. Willard had apparently not revived sufficiently to serve us, for it was Shiftwell who handed around the plates.

"What a night it was, to be sure!" Rachel was saying. "I shall never forget it. My first thought on hearing of the invasion was for the safety of your team and carriage, Aiglon. I trust there is nothing amiss with them?"

His expression was remarkably ungrateful. "Nothing irreparable, my groom tells me. He has a fomentation on that sprained foreleg. At least Willard hadn't strength enough to destroy their mouths. The wheeler is coming to put on a new wheel and repair the cracked axle."

I looked fearfully at Rachel during this litany of complaints, but she was only nodding her head. "How soon do you think we can get away to Westleigh?" she asked when he had finished.

"In a day or two if all goes well," Aiglon replied.

"Shall I join you, milord, or will you want me to return to London to handle things there?" Retchling asked.

"Oh, you must come with us, Riddell," Rachel exclaimed. I wasn't surprised to have his name confirmed, but I was a little surprised to hear Rachel utter it so matter-of-factly.

"When did you change your name, Beau?" I asked.

"Never, ma'am," he answered. "We selected the nickname of Beau as it is the one my friends in London call me. As to the other Retchling, he will be *aux anges* to learn he starred in a *divertissement*. I expect he'll write it all up in a story or drama, don't you, Aiglon?"

"Not at all. It's too long for a *pensée*. He hasn't the staying power for anything beyond five lines."

"I don't quite see the necessity for calling yourself anything other than Mr. Riddell," Rachel said, her tone inviting an explanation. "I understand your letting on to be in the basket, Aiglon, to encourage the disreputable element to approach you. I daresay Mickey never would have opened up to a perfectly respectable gentleman, but why did Mr. Riddell have to assume an alias?"

The gentlemen exchanged a meaningful glance. "That was another matter entirely, ma'am," Riddell answered vaguely.

"What matter was that?" Rachel persisted.

I began to suspect that Riddell had come in disguise to investigate the irregularities in Rachel's housekeeping practices. She would not have been so forthcoming to Riddell as she had been to Retchling. She was swift enough that she soon tumbled to it herself and quitted the subject adroitly.

"I'm so happy your team and carriage suffered no serious damage, Aiglon. I would never have forgiven myself if I'd left them to Boney and taken my own horses instead. But then you know I always put your welfare before my own. I consider it all part and parcel of being your housekeeper."

"I don't see why you didn't take both carriages," Riddell mentioned.

"Yes, particularly since Constance was left to walk," Aiglon threw in.

"I certainly assumed Constance would have the wits to harness up the other carriage, but we shan't be too hard on her. You've no idea of the pandemonium caused in the countryside when you had those stacks lit, Aiglon. I'll be mighty surprised if you haven't a life or two to account for. I know I very nearly died of fright." These misleading statements were listened to in stony silence.

Next she was rattling on about the matter of Aiglon's having put Thornbury up for sale. "You really must speak to Roundtree about that before you leave, or Constance and I will have the nuisance of turning people away at the door.''

''Constance won't be here, Rachel, but in fact I didn't actually put Thornbury on the block. I only discussed it with Roundtree,'' Aiglon told her.

''Constance not here? My dear girl, you're not leaving me! Is it because of Prissy's having nabbed a fellow? Are you needed at home?'' she asked.

''No, it is because of Constance's having nabbed one, I believe,'' Riddell said, casting a mischievous smile on Aiglon and myself.

I felt a perfect fool. Aiglon had not mentioned the word *marriage* yet. I had some hopes that he would, but to be on the verge of receiving congratulations so prematurely was embarrassing.

''I *did* write to Papa when Aiglon spoke of selling Thornbury,'' I said, my face glowing red.

''Then it's all right. You won't have to leave,'' Rachel decided, and fanned herself with her napkin. The suggestion that I had nabbed Aiglon bothered her, however, and she rattled on to make my ineligibility clear. She let on it was Riddell himself who was interested in me. ''I'm sure Aiglon couldn't part with you, Riddell. And, of course, you and Constance couldn't both live with him. Lady Aiglon wouldn't care for that! So charming, your dear mama, Aiglon, but very high in the instep, is she not?''

''Not at all,'' Aiglon answered blandly. ''And she doesn't live with me, either. She usually visits me in London for a month or so during the Season, but at Westleigh she lives in the Dower House.''

''Still, I think Mr. Riddell had better find himself another bride.''

Aiglon smiled and shook his head. ''She's right, you

know, Beau. You really must stop making up to Miss Pethel behind my back. Find your own girl.''

Rachel was on thorns to get me alone and squeeze the truth out of me. Her concern, of course, was that I was too well informed on the details of her housekeeping. She wouldn't relish that knowledge in Aiglon's wife. The gentlemen drove into town to speak with Cokewell, and Rachel came hounding after me in the garden.

''What nonsense is this about your having set up a flirtation with Aiglon, Constance?'' she demanded, her nose slipping chinward.

''I didn't set up any flirtation! But Aiglon does seem rather . . . fond of me,'' I admitted.

''He is fond of every chit he meets, providing she isn't downright ugly. He'll forget you soon enough once he returns to London. I would hate to see you hurt, Constance. Pray don't look for anything from that quarter.'' After this motherly advice, she asked bluntly, ''Has he spoken to you?''

I smiled confidently and answered, ''No. Not yet.''

I could see her mind at work. Her eyes settled at a spot behind the rosebushes, and she said, ''When you wrote to your papa, did you ask him to come for you?''

''I said I would like to go home, yes,'' I told her.

''Take my carriage,'' she offered at once. ''There's no point in delaying your return. You wouldn't care for Westleigh in the least. A great, drafty heap of a place in the wilds of nowhere.''

''I'm used to drafty heaps in the wilds of nowhere, Rachel. I shan't mind it. Excuse me, but I must go and see to my packing now.''

I didn't see her again until luncheon, and by that time the gentlemen had returned from Folkestone and joined us at the table.

"What's new in town?" Rachel asked. She was trying to behave normally, but her nose had taken up permanent residence at a low point on her face.

"The whole world is packing up its valuables and hiding them," Aiglon said.

"Hiding them where?" I inquired.

"Where the Frenchies won't find them if they invade," Aiglon explained. "Naturally, every family is exercising some secrecy with regard to the hiding spot to prevent local theft, but it seems some folks are burying them in gardens and orchards and things. Of course it's an old tradition in England. Much the same thing was done in Cromwell's day. There are any number of legends of buried treasure in old homes such as this one. If the burier happened to get himself killed without telling anyone where the riches were hidden, the new owner had to try to divine the spot."

"There's some such legend about Thornbury, isn't there?" Beau asked innocently. He didn't look at Aiglon, but I had the impression of a strong current of meaning between them all the same.

I glanced at Rachel and noticed that she was wadding her napkin into a ball between her fingers. "All a hum," she said firmly. But those twisting fingers did not denote disbelief. I suddenly knew what secret was in the gray book. She had discovered that there was hidden treasure at Thornbury. She had read that it was buried in or near some small stone building separate from but close to the main house. She had thought it was the chapel, but her diggings there had not revealed the secret. It was Mickey who had learned the legend in that old book, and he had quizzed Rachel, perhaps trying to learn some of the history of the place so that he would know where to dig. She'd managed to find out about the book and bought it before he could.

The greatest surprise was that Mickey had let her get such a jump on him, but I imagine he only mentioned the story in passing, taking it for an unfounded tale. It was odd that she was so eager to get to Westleigh with a buried treasure waiting to be discovered. I thought I must be wrong until I remembered a chance statement of Aiglon's. Something about some old records at Westleigh. The records at Thornbury were few and incomplete. The greater part of the ancient library had been taken to Westleigh when the family first removed there.

When I returned my attention to the table, Aiglon was relating some other goings-on in town. "Cokewell is distributing the guns to the militiamen," he was saying. "He's called an emergency session tonight to teach the men how to load and fire them. They were setting up targets on the Leas when we were there."

"Thank God we're far enough away we won't hear the racket of hundreds of guns going off," Rachel said. "What's the word on Madame Bieler?"

"She's been taken to London under close guard. Mick is looking pretty down in the mouth," Aiglon said. "I mean to speak to Lord Ware when I return to London and ask him to find a position for Dougherty there, away from the mischief of smuggling."

"What will we do for silks if he goes?" Rachel objected.

"Someone will replace Mick, never fear. Madame and Mick aren't the only entrepreneurs in town. There's already talk of Miss Calisher taking over Madame's shop."

"Miss Calisher!" Rachel exclaimed. "She is the vicar's sister! Surely she's not thinking of setting up a shop and selling contraband."

"No, no, I misled you. She is only going to be the modiste. Someone less nice will take over the selling of the contraband silk and brandy, I expect," Aiglon explained.

"There must be a wicked profit in it," Rachel said. Her face wore a different look now. It was the calculating look that came when she discovered a new way to weasel money out of Aiglon. I had an intuition that before long it would be Rachel herself who was doling out the delightful silks. I also had a strong feeling there would be an increase in the price.

When Rachel decided to take a run into Folkestone without asking me along, I knew I was right. She was going to arrange it with Mickey Dougherty, but I didn't care. It left me free to be with Aiglon.

He got rid of Riddell by asking him to go and speak to the wheeler about the carriage. Riddell gave us a knowing look. "And what shall I say, milord? Shall I repeat the message given by your groom a few hours ago?"

"That will be fine, Beau."

"Would it serve as well if I removed myself to the study?"

"When I said go, I only meant away. *You* choose the destination," Aiglon replied sardonically.

"As you wish, milord. Shall I prepare a letter to Mr. Pethel while there, or would you prefer to write it yourself?"

"Just leave room for my signature. You will do a better job of puffing me up than modesty would permit me to do."

While Riddell was still there smirking at us, Aiglon turned from him and pretended to think that he had gone. "Other people have the pleasure of hiding their skeletons in the closet. Mine follows at my heels like a demmed puppy. Riddell is one of my disreputable relations. We all have our dirty dishes. Riddell, like his alter ego, Retchling, is a genius, you see. A first at Oxford, a translation of

Ovid into nearly readable English, and now at last he has risen to the eminence of being my man of business. Ah, are you still here, Beau?"

"No, milord. I left several lies ago. It was a *double* first at Oxford, and it was Virgil whom I rendered into entirely readable English. Some discerning critics called it inspired."

"They would be the ones who didn't read it but based their critiques on the expensive leather binding. Thank you, Beau. I'll frank the letter as soon as you've gotten around to writing it. I imagine they hide the paper and ink in the study here. Rachel is so unimaginative in matters that don't involve money."

Beau smiled and left. "You're rather hard on him!" I objected.

"Only to lengthen his life. His head has a tendency to swell when he's performed well. He performed well in this past scrape and needs deflating before he explodes. Shall we retire to our rocks?"

"Yes, I'm curious to investigate and see just how much digging Mickey has actually done," I answered.

"Only three holes so far. He had a go at the sacristy and just beyond the walls."

"Oh, you know all about it! How did you find out?"

We went out into the afternoon sunlight and meandered through the garden toward the chapel.

"Beau was helpful in purloining Rachel's gray book. There's no truth in the old tale, but it kept Mickey in line to let him think he had a fortune at his fingertips. We discussed the other part of his bribe, you recall? It was nip and tuck for a while whether he'd throw in his lot with Madame or me. As well as her delightful self, she has some holdings in Ireland that were a troublesome lure, but the ingenious Beau convinced Mick he was sitting on a barrel of rubies and diamonds here, so we snagged him for our side.''

"How do you know the story's not true?" I asked.

"I don't actually *know* it. I *do* know that every inhabitant since Cromwell's time has had a go at finding the jewelry without luck. In any case, it will keep Rachel out of our hair at Westleigh, going over the old documents. And if she finds anything, so much the better. We'll let her dig it up and then claim it for our own.''

"You're as bad as she is!"

"Worse, dear heart,'' he warned, offering me a stone seat. "She was only interested in borrowing you for a few years and making you her unpaid companion and part-time lackey. *I* plan to steal you permanently, body and soul.''

The air caught in my lungs when I saw the love glowing in his eyes. It didn't seem possible that it was happening, that this hero had come and found me in the wilds of Thornbury. That I was to be swept off to Westleigh and London to share in his life.

"Do you think your mama will . . . I mean, Rachel seemed to think . . .''

"Rachel knows Mama will love you, as I do. Not exactly as I do, of course, but Rachel was only fearful of what housekeeping secrets you might tell me. Quite frankly, I'm not at all interested in that. It's Riddell she'll have to deal with if she plans to stay on here till Nick returns. And I think, and hope, the lure of lining her pockets from brandy and silk might encourage her to stay.''

"I thought the same thing even before you mentioned it.''

"It is said that when a man and a woman begin communicating without the need of words, they should either stop seeing each other or get married.''

As he spoke, his arms pulled me to him. "I never heard that before.''

"Neither did I. I just made it up now," he admitted, planting a fleeting kiss on my nose. "So which is it to be, my flower? Do I leave you at Thornbury to Rachel's tender care or steal you from her?"

His lips were tracing a warm path along my jawbone, down the length of my neck, making speech nearly impossible for the quivering, choking sensation that came over me.

"It's rather dangerous here with Boney just across the Channel," I said, my voice shaking most unnaturally. "It would be good to get away."

"I never thought I'd have anything to thank Napoleon Bonaparte for!" he scowled.

"Of course you have. If it hadn't been for Boney, you'd never have come here at all, Aiglon. I've been here for five years, hearing about you, and . . ."

"What has she told you? It's not true, Constance!"

"You mean Westleigh *isn't* the prettiest heap in Hampshire? You *don't* have a fine home in the city as well, and ten thousand a year? What a plumper! Here I set my cap at a nobody. I might as well have stayed home and married the cobbler." I pulled free from him and sat on the rock, thinking he would sit beside me, but he didn't.

"Ah, well, if that was the nature of her talk, of course she's absolutely right. She couldn't lie if her life depended on it. And you *didn't* set your cap at me. That's what first attracted my attention to you. Why did you not?"

"I was forewarned! Rachel, who is incapable of a lie, cautioned me as to your wandering ways."

"Did she, by God? The woman's a witch, I swear. She knew I would fall in love with you and wanted to prevent the match." He spoke lightly, but when he stopped, a more serious expression settled on him. "I can't claim a saintly background for myself, Constance. There have been a few women, but none of them . . ."

He stopped and smiled softly. "None of them were *you*. After my younger brother went off to the Peninsula, I began to take stock of my worthless life and mended my ways. I took the job at the F.O. to do my bit for the war. It gave me a great sense of satisfaction until that load of arms went astray under my responsibility. I decided then to resuscitate my old reputation for wildness and track them down. I thought I might find my way into the gang more readily if I were spoken of as a worthless fellow in need of quick money. So I called myself the opponent in Kirkwell's duel to give me an excuse for coming here at this rather daunting time when anyone with a particle of sense was leaving the coast. The loss of one shipment might not have been worth so much effort, but as they got clean away with one, we feared they might go after others. So I had my superior write up that letter implying I was turned off from the F.O. Then an unexpected but perfectly delightful complication turned up. *You,*" he said. "I suddenly discovered that I didn't want to be known as a scoundrel and a drunkard. I wanted to show you my better side, but without changing my colors enough to tip Mickey the clue. Shakespeare, another genius, said it best. 'We that are true lovers run into strange capers.' It's been a strange caper."

"Does that mean we're true lovers then?"

"I've been looking for a lady worthy of true love and have found her. You must speak for yourself." He stood, looking at me with a very flattering uncertainty that soon turned to impatience. "Well?" he asked.

"I never argue with Shakespeare, and I've been somewhat involved in the caper, too. But *true* lovers cannot lie as you do, Aiglon."

A slow smile spread across his face as he pulled me up from the rock and into his arms. "Why, you said yourself lies aren't lies when Aiglon tells them. Don't be pedantic," he added, closing my lips with a finger to silence my objection. "Even if I was forced to tamper with the truth, I mean to keep my promise to find you a husband."

"On your word of honor?"

"Word of a gentleman, and a liar," he assured me, but his kiss had the *feeling* of truth. That was all I knew, or needed to know.

There's an epidemic with 27 million victims. And no visible symptoms.

It's an epidemic of people who can't read.

Believe it or not, 27 million Americans are functionally illiterate, about one adult in five.

The solution to this problem is you... when you join the fight against illiteracy. So call the Coalition for Literacy at toll-free **1-800-228-8813** and volunteer.

**Volunteer
Against Illiteracy.
The only degree you need
is a degree of caring.**

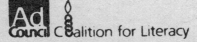

Ad Council Coalition for Literacy

LV-1